HARLEQUIN®
Presents

Fantastic Stories for Fall!

Emma Darcy is back with *The Playboy Boss's Chosen Bride,* the story of arrogant Jake Devila and Merlina, who grabs her chance to make him see that she's not just his dowdy, reliable secretary. Penny Jordan is on sizzling form with *Master of Pleasure*: Sasha thought she'd walked away from Gabriel Cabrini, but now he possesses her once more. Julia James guarantees dark desire in *Purchased for Revenge*: Greek tycoon Alexei Constantin has only one thing on his mind—vengeance. If that means bedding Eve he'll do it. Jane Porter delivers drama, glamour and intense emotion when Spanish superstar Wolf Kerrick claims Alexandra, his rags-to-riches bride, in *Hollywood Husband, Contract Wife*. For a touch of regal romance, choose *The Rich Man's Royal Mistress,* the second part of Robyn Donald's trilogy, THE ROYAL HOUSE OF ILLYRIA. Virginal Princess Melissa falls under the spell of man-of-the-world billionaire Hawke Kennedy. In Elizabeth Power's compelling *The Millionaire's Love-Child,* Annie and former boss, Brant Cadman, are reunited in a marriage of convenience when they discover that their babies were swapped at birth. While Anton, the Comte de Valois, demands that Diana become his bride when she becomes pregnant. But what is behind his proposal? Find out in *The French Count's Pregnant Bride* by Catherine Spencer. Bought and bedded by the sheikh—the explosive passion between Prince Malik and Abbie could turn an arranged marriage into one of Eastern delight in Kate Walker's *At the Sheikh's Command.*

Legally wed,
but he's never said,
"I love you."
They're...

The series where marriages are made
in haste...and love comes later....

Look out for more WEDLOCKED!
wedding stories. Available only from
Harlequin Presents®.

Elizabeth Power

THE MILLIONAIRE'S LOVE-CHILD

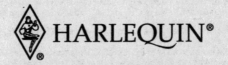

TORONTO • NEW YORK • LONDON
AMSTERDAM • PARIS • SYDNEY • HAMBURG
STOCKHOLM • ATHENS • TOKYO • MILAN • MADRID
PRAGUE • WARSAW • BUDAPEST • AUCKLAND

ISBN-13: 978-0-373-12577-7
ISBN-10:   0-373-12577-1

THE MILLIONAIRE'S LOVE-CHILD

First North American Publication 2006.

Copyright © 2004 by Elizabeth Power.

This edition published by arrangement with Harlequin Books S.A.

® and TM are trademarks of the publisher. Trademarks indicated with ® are registered in the United States Patent and Trademark Office, the Canadian Trade Marks Office and in other countries.

www.eHarlequin.com

Printed in U.S.A.

All about the author...
Elizabeth Power

ELIZABETH POWER was born in Bristol, where
she still lives with her husband in a 300-year-old
cottage. A keen reader, as a teenager she had already
made up her mind to be a novelist. But it wasn't
until a few weeks before her thirtieth birthday that
Elizabeth was thinking about what she had done
with her first thirty years, and realized she had been
telling herself she would "start writing tomorrow" for
at least twelve of them and took up writing seriously.
Within two weeks the letter that was to change her
life arrived from Harlequin. *Rude Awakening* was
to be published in 1986. After a prolonged absence,
Elizabeth is pleased to be back at her keyboard again,
and with new romances already in the works.

Emotional intensity is paramount in her books. She
says "times, places and trends change, but emotion
is timeless." A powerful story line with maximum
emotion set in a location in which you can really
live and breathe while the story unfolds is what she
strives for. Good food and wine come high on her
list of priorities, and what better way to sample
these delights than by just having to take another trip
to some new exotic resort. Oh, and of course
to find a location for the next book!

CHAPTER ONE

'No, NO! It's not true! I don't believe you!'

Annie swung away, towards the window, her bare shoulders stiffening in rejection of the man's devastating statement. Beneath the dark strands of her fringe, bewildered brown eyes stared out on the small square of garden that formed the rear of her terraced London flat, at the low boundary wall where the long-haired tabby crouched, poised to eject any other exploring cat from its territory. 'You've got to be joking. Tell me it's just some cruel joke. That you're making it up. You are, aren't you?'

'I'm sorry, Annie.' Behind her, those deep masculine tones were soft, yet unrelenting. 'If I could have found an easier way to tell you, believe me, I would have.'

'Don't you think I'd *know*?' Her thick layered hair bounced against her shoulders as she pivoted to face the man again, disbelief and confusion stamped on the pale oval of her face.

For a few seconds her eyes read—what? Sympathy, in the green-gold depths of his? Some emotion that softened those angular features with their forceful jaw and that hawk-like nose which, with his sleek black hair and the immaculate tailoring of his dark suit, added up to an almost intimidating presence. 'Don't you think I'd have realised if a mistake like that had been made? Do you think I wouldn't know my own child?'

'Annie. Annie...' His hand outstretched, he made a move towards her, but she recoiled from any contact, shivering suddenly beneath her scanty purple sun-top and jeans. 'You're in shock.'

'What do you expect?' she flung at him, backing away from any further attempt to console her. How could he offer any consolation except to retract what he had just said?

Broad shoulders sagged almost indiscernibly beneath the well-cut jacket, and his breath came heavily as he said, 'Don't you think that this has been hard for me?'

She could see the lines now at the corners of those beautiful eyes, and the way his smooth, olive skin seemed stretched across his cheekbones from battle-scarring emotions made him appear even fiercer than when she had known him before. If, of course, she could claim to have known him before. She had, after all, been just a cog in the running of his empire.

Brant Cadman. Thirty-five years old and the driving force behind Cadman Leisure, whose name was synonymous with a whole chain of retail outlets, sports complexes and manufacturers of his own brand of sportswear, including the company where she had worked with Warren. But that was before she had paid the price of trusting someone. Before she had felt the need to leave her job, stung by the shame of everyone knowing. Before she had had her son.

And here Brant was, saying that the child she had raised for the past two years wasn't her child at all, but his. His and some other woman's. That the hospital where his own son had been born had found a discrepancy in their records which had only come to light following advisory blood tests after both he and the boy had been exposed to some viral infection during a recent visit to Spain.

Hot tears burned Annie's eyes now, the long strands of her fringe tangling with her equally long lashes as she shook her head in denial.

'No, no. It isn't true! Sean's mine! He's always been mine!' In all her twenty-five years she could never have imagined being dealt a blow like this.

As she swayed she saw Brant glance swiftly around, grab

the chair beside the second-hand table where her paints and brushes and the miniature water-colour she was working on lay. He set it down beside her, exerting gentle pressure on her shoulder as he urged, 'Annie, sit down.'

Like an automaton, she obeyed, too numb to do anything else.

'When they told me, I didn't want to believe it either.' His voice was raw with the intensity of anguish he had obviously suffered—was still suffering—because of it. 'But as soon as you opened the door to me, there wasn't any doubt.'

What was he saying? Her face tilted swiftly to his, pain warring with incomprehension. That the child he was raising, whose existence until a few moments ago she had never given more than a passing thought to, somehow resembled her? Was actually *hers*?

She shook her head again. It wasn't possible. The child slumbering in the next room, obliviously peaceful in his afternoon nap—he was hers. Sean was her baby.

'OK. So the baby you thought was yours and your wife's suddenly isn't. But what makes you think Sean's yours?' Numbness and shock were giving way to a challenging anger. 'What makes you think you can come here and try to take my baby away? Did the hospital send you? Did they tell you to come here?'

'No.' He slipped his hands into his pockets, his pristine white shirt pulled tautly across his chest, as though he'd taken a breath and forgotten to let it out. 'And the last thing I want to do,' he said quietly, 'is take your baby away.'

Annie took a gulp of air. She, too, was finding it difficult to breathe. 'You can try,' she dared him vehemently.

He chose to ignore the challenge. 'The hospital called me in when they found Jack's blood type didn't match up with the record they had on computer. They confirmed from their records of Naomi's blood group and now my own that we couldn't have produced a child with the same type as Jack's. There was only one baby born that day two years ago whose details show up as having the correct blood type for any child of ours. Yours Annie. The only conclusion they could come to was that some time before our babies left the hospital, there had been a switch.'

'No. It's all a mistake! They had no right to give you my name!'

'They didn't,' he said, looking down at his feet. 'They said they couldn't divulge the identity of our son's—as they called it—"biological mother".'

Biological mother?

A low moan, that could have come from her own throat rang out from the direction of the garden. An ominous sound presaging a bitter conflict, a struggle from which only the strongest and most determined could emerge unscathed.

'So what led you here?' Had he known two years ago that Annie Talbot—poor jilted Annie, his ex-employee—had given birth on the same day as his wife? Because *she* hadn't. Not until afterwards. Not until a friend had told her that Naomi Cadman had died within twenty-four hours of producing a son. 'No one's contacted me. Wouldn't they have done if these ludicrous assumptions of yours were true?'

'They should have. They said they were doing so.' His hands dropped from his pockets. 'And they aren't assumptions, Annie. I wish they were. It's fact—yet to be confirmed, but from the hospital itself.'

'But…you said they wouldn't give out information, that it was against their—'

'They didn't. Not knowingly. When they called me in, I was left alone in the office for a short spell. The computer was on. I'd have to be superhuman not to have given in to the need to know.'

'So you scrolled through the records?' Eyes accusing, she

wanted to rush to the phone. Report him. Tell them he'd picked her name from a whole host of others who could have given birth that day.

'No, Annie. I merely strode over to look at it from the other side of the desk. Your details were on the screen. I suppose such carelessness is hardly surprising from an establishment that sends parents home with the wrong children.'

The wrong children. His words, and the anger that infiltrated them, was bringing her to the slow and awful realisation that it might possibly be true. That Sean, whom she loved and cherished more than life itself, might not be hers. That she might suddenly find herself in a long, traumatic battle to keep him.

Through the open window came a sudden low chorus of howls.

'They didn't have your correct address on record. I only found this place through Katrina King.' From his rather dubious glance around her modest little flat he didn't need to tell her what he thought about it. 'I seem to recall you being close friends when you worked at Cadman Sport.'

So he had remembered that. And he had gone to great lengths to find her, even looking up the only friend and colleague she kept in touch with from her old job.

'Have you had your son DNA-tested? Or whatever it is they do to ascertain parenthood these days? Is that why you're so certain your little boy's been mixed up with mine?'

She couldn't help the scorn in her voice, betraying the hurt and the anger she was suddenly feeling, not so much with him but with the hospital and those people responsible for placing her—placing all of them—in such a harrowing situation.

'No, I haven't.' He looked down at his sleek black polished shoes again. 'Yet.'

'Why not?' The question seemed torn from her, but then she read the answer in those green-gold eyes. He wanted to know. Of course he did. But likewise, he didn't want to know. And it struck her then, in startling clarity, the implications that such a test could lead to. Because if his boy wasn't the baby that Naomi had given birth to...

She froze, staring at the table with her palette and her paints and all the colourful trappings that made up her world and provided her with an income and stability. She'd want to know, and yet would balk from the truth just as Brant was doing. She couldn't bear ever to know for certain that Sean wasn't her son.

A small sound from the adjoining room had her jumping up instinctively. Their voices—or the cat's howls—had woken him. But not for long. He was quiet again, still sleeping as she opened the brightly painted door to peer through the crack, then closed it again.

'Can I see him?'

She swung round, gasping at finding Brant standing right behind her. At five feet four she suddenly felt dwarfed by his six-foot-plus frame.

'No!' Her arms flew out across the door-well, and above her panicked response she heard a sudden skirmish outside. Bouncer defending his territory, protecting all he valued, all that was his. 'No, not now,' she enlarged in what she hoped was a more conciliatory tone.

The light from the window struck fire from the man's hair as he dipped his head. 'I understand.'

Did he? From the taut lines of that fiercely chiselled face she understood herself that he was exercising a formidable restraint. This close to him, she caught the elusive scent of the cologne he must have used that morning; could almost feel the tangible warmth emanating from his hard body. And rising through the trauma of the moment was the shocking recognition of his flagrant sexuality, the memory of how once, too inexperienced to resist it, she had made a total fool of herself with this man.

But that was ten lifetimes ago, she told herself. Before he had relinquished his glorious bachelordom and married the sophisticated Naomi Fox.

She wondered if he was remembering it too, or even if—heaven forbid!—he was aware of her raging emotions, before he took a couple of steps back, giving her space: cool, remote, detached. When he had telephoned earlier he had warned her that this wasn't exactly a social call, the simple statement assuring her, as it was probably meant to, that whatever had happened between them in the past was just that—in the past.

'I can get you counselling,' he said. 'It was offered to me.'

But you refused it. Of course you did, she thought, certain that no one could direct or analyse the thoughts and feelings of Brant Cadman better than Brant Cadman himself.

She lifted her hands, palms upwards, as though she was fending off something threatening, saying disjointedly, 'I...don't need counselling. I just...want you to go.'

'I don't think you should be left alone.' His face was grim with concern.

'I'm not alone. I've got Sean.' Her chin lifted with determined ferocity. 'I don't care if it's true—what you say. I won't be giving him up.'

He seemed about to say something else, perhaps to contest her remark, but then his lips compressed on whatever it was, and he said, 'I want what's best for Jack—as I'm sure you do for Sean. I appreciate that this has been a terrible shock and that you need time for it to sink in. But there are things we have to discuss. Work out. I'd like to come back tomorrow.'

She knew she couldn't deny him that if what he was

saying was true. Nevertheless, a deep, resisting fear showed in her velvet-brown eyes.

'It's all right, Annie.' His gaze raked over the anxious lines of her face with its pert nose, softly defined mouth and the gentle curvature of her jaw. Briefly his eyes shaped the long line of her throat and the smooth slope of her shoulders, gently tanned from minutes snatched in the early-June sun, and, lifting his gaze back to hers, he said softly, 'Are you going to be all right?'

She nodded, but thought, What does he care? He's only interested in his son. Or who he thinks is his son.

Panic brought her into the bedroom after she had shown him out.

In his little bed, Sean was stirring, wisps of nut-brown hair highlighted against the white pillow. The cats might have disturbed him earlier, but everything was quiet now. Through the little lace curtain she could see Bouncer preening himself further along the wall, smug in his obvious victory.

She wondered what her parents would think if they had been here today. But they were twelve thousand miles away in New Zealand.

Over three years ago, when her architect father had taken early retirement and he and his wife had decided to emigrate, they had wanted Annie to go with them. At the time, however, she had just fallen madly in love with Warren Maddox. It had been a whirlwind romance. A time of foolish dreams, planning for a wedding that was to take place only six months after their first meeting. When he had jilted her for Caroline Fenn, an up-and-coming model he'd met on one of the firm's promotional assignments only two weeks before the wedding, Jane and Simon Talbot had begged Annie to join them, but determinedly she had declined. She was fine, she had told them, wanting to carry on with her life, pretend nothing had happened. In truth, she had been dealt such a blow that she had just wanted to remain alone to lick her wounds.

When she had had Sean, however, against her protests, her mother had made the long journey to be with her, over-protective, fussing in her well-meaning way, so that it was with mixed emotions, two weeks later, that Annie had seen her off on her journey home. Six months later she had taken Sean and flown over to spend Christmas in Auckland with them, returning after a month. That was nearly eighteen months ago.

Now Annie had to quell the strongest urge to ring her parents, hear her father's understanding tones, but it would be the middle of the night in New Zealand and she had never been one to run for help at the first sign of trouble.

As Sean's hazel eyes opened and he gave her a wide grin, adoringly Annie picked him up. He felt cuddly and warm in his soft pyjamas.

Everything would be sorted out, she tried convincing herself. He had her father's ears, didn't he? And everyone said he had her cheeky smile and her colouring.

But as she looked at the child in her arms, reminding herself of all these things, all she could see was the strong, daunting features of Brant Cadman.

The letter came from the hospital the following morning. It told Annie to contact them as soon as possible.

When she rang they said they wanted to send someone out to see her. Perhaps the following day? But Annie insisted that if they had something to tell her, she was coming up to town herself. Today.

She didn't tell them that she knew what it concerned. Or anything about Brant Cadman. Ridiculously, she was nursing the hope that if she didn't bring his name into it, this whole harrowing nightmare might not be true.

For what other reason the hospital might be writing to

her, she didn't stop to imagine. The fact that Brant had said he would be calling round again today was very real and she was keen to get out of the flat before he arrived. She didn't think she could face him until someone told her for certain that there had been a mix-up. Until then, he presented a dark threat to everything she cherished.

'I take it you know Brant Cadman was here,' Katrina King told her as soon as Annie rang to ask her friend if she would have Sean for a couple of hours. A year older than Annie, the woman worked from home as a freelance sportswear designer. She loved children and had volunteered to entertain Sean if ever Annie needed a babysitter. 'You did get my email, didn't you?'

She hadn't. She'd been too worried and overtaken by the man's visit to even remember to check her emails.

'When did he call?' was all Annie could respond with.

'About coffee-time yesterday. Still looking like every woman's darkest fantasy. What did he want?' Katrina asked, sounding suspicious.

'Just to see me,' Annie returned, thinking how pretentious that sounded, but at that moment she couldn't begin to tell her friend the nature of Brant's visit.

'I'll bet!' Katrina's words held a mixture of caution and envy, but Annie ignored them.

'See you later,' she said quickly, ringing off.

She didn't want to let Sean out of her sight, but decided it would be best if he was with Katrina. Her friend only lived a short drive away, and fifteen minutes later, with Sean safely delivered into the woman's care, Annie was driving back through the suburbs only to realise that, with all the trauma of what was happening, she had forgotten both the letter from the hospital and the name of the person she was supposed to see.

Forced to make a detour back to the flat, she was tripping down the steps again to her little purple Ka when she saw

the dark blue Mercedes saloon suddenly pulling up in front
of her home.

Brant Cadman! She didn't even need to look at the driver
to know it would be him. Not too many cars of that sort
parked outside her modest little address!

She felt her whole body tense as he unfolded himself
from the big car.

'Good morning.'

Somehow, Annie found her tongue to acknowledge him
and felt his eyes flit over her, noticing, no doubt, the sharp
rise and fall of her small breasts in response to seeing him
standing there.

'Are you going out?'

Of course, he would want to know, she thought with her
stomach knotting, struck by how devastating he looked in
his casual grey polo shirt and pale chinos. But that was what
men like Brant Cadman did. Devastate.

'That letter came today.' She started towards the Ka. 'I'm
going to the hospital.' She couldn't have lied to him even
if she had wanted to and was suddenly disconcerted to find
his tall, lean frame blocking her path.

'Then get into the car.' He was indicating his own plush
saloon. 'We'll go together.'

'No!' Even to her own ears she sounded like a frightened
schoolgirl.

'Annie!' His sigh was exasperated. 'The last thing I want
to do is hurt you.'

He meant emotionally, she thought, but he had already
done that.

'I just need to do this alone. To be alone.' It wasn't meant
to, but it came out as a plea.

'You won't want to, Annie. Not afterwards,' he assured
her softly.

He had been through it already, she remembered. But just
because he had been sent home with the wrong baby, it

didn't mean for certain that she had, did it? So he had got her name off the computer. So she had been in the hospital giving birth at the same time as his wife. But so had a number of other women, probably. And blood tests weren't a hundred per cent accurate, were they? Sean couldn't be the only baby that the Cadman boy could have been switched with. Could he?

The anguish that accompanied her silent, tortured questions momentarily disarmed her, leaving her open to his decisive will.

'Come on. I'll drive you,' he stated. And that was that.

Her tension might have got the better of her, holding her rigid as a statue for most of the journey. But Brant kept her talking so that she couldn't spend the whole of the drive dwelling on the traumatic situation, something deliberately calculated to relax her, she was sure.

Only once did she feel the sickening dread in the pit of her stomach threaten to overwhelm her, and that was at the outset when he asked, 'Where's Sean?'

'I thought it best that he didn't come.' Annie's tone was defensive. 'He's at Katrina's.'

She was expecting some demand from him to see the son he claimed was his, but all he said was, 'You get on well with her. Where did the two of you meet? At Cadman Sport?'

'No. We were at art college together. She left before me, then told me about the vacancy in the art department, and so I joined too.'

She was aware of him steering the powerful car through the heavy traffic, of the courtesy he extended to other drivers as he slowed to let someone out of a side-turning.

'What do you do now?'

'I sell miniature water-colours to anyone who'll take them, basically.' She had a couple of regular outlets. A small gallery in Essex. A tea-shop selling crafts in a smaller village out of town.

'Is it rewarding?'

She glanced at him, pulling a face. 'You mean financially?' That sort of thing, she thought, would probably rank as a priority to a man like him.

But he said, 'Not necessarily,' slowing down to stop at a red light.

'You mean spiritually?' Annie's dark lashes shot up under the strands of her fringe. 'As food for my well-being?'

'Don't knock it,' he said, wise to the hint of surprised cynicism she had directed towards him. 'Isn't that the most important form of reward?'

'Yes, it is,' she answered, to both his questions, because financially she only just scraped a living at present, and she certainly didn't intend going back to work for anyone else yet and leaving Sean with strangers. She had decided from the beginning that she would look after her baby herself.

Her baby. And now here was Brant, driving her to an interview that might rob her of the right to call him that forever.

No! Panic brought on that queasy feeling again with sickening intensity, draining the colour from her cheeks.

The sun struck the polished bonnet of the car, hurting her eyes with its remorseless glare. Her head tilted to one side to avoid it, as Brant put the car in motion again, she didn't even see him glance her way.

'Are you all right?' he asked quietly.

Annie shot a look at his harshly defined profile. 'Sure. I feel great! How do you expect me to feel?' She felt too hurt, too angry, too everything to avoid making the challenge. For the briefest moment, as he turned his head, she noticed the deep concern in his eyes.

''Course.' His jaw seemed clenched as his attention returned to the road. 'Stupid question.'

'I'm sorry.' It was all she could say to excuse herself. She was too strung up, as well as much too conscious of him sitting beside her: of those long-tapered fingers as they flicked on the indicator, of the latent strength of his hair-furred arm as he turned the wheel.

When he glanced at her again, it was with more than just concern.

'What?' Annie prompted, aware.

'The first time I saw you,' he responded with a slight smile curving his mouth, 'you were wearing that colour.' His gaze fell briefly on the royal-blue top that shaped her upper body, and which clung to her tiny waist above the wide cream belt hugging her hips. 'You seemed to epitomise everything that was bright and young and vibrant. You were wearing a vivid blue blouse with a tight black skirt and at least four-inch-high heels that made me wonder how you could even stand in them, let alone hold yourself with such alluring dignity.'

He hadn't been able to take his eyes off her, she remembered, shocked even now to recognise the depth of excitement his interest had produced in her. But that was when she had been guileless, unaware of how easily a man could pledge his feelings, and how easily a woman could be snared by her own sexuality. That was when she had still been young enough to take her happiness as read, before Warren had jilted her, before she had reacted to his defection to his lovely model in the most humiliating way.

'I suppose practice makes perfect,' she said tartly, and wondered, with a sudden quickening of her pulse, if despite his marriage and all the time that had passed since, he could still be remotely attracted to her.

Then she decided it was just another ploy on his part to take her mind off the main issue when, still thinking about a whole host of things she would have been wise not to remember, she heard him say, 'Here we are.'

CHAPTER TWO

IF SHE lived to be a hundred and fifty, Annie thought, she wouldn't have believed it possible to find herself a victim of such a bizarre and cruel coincidence.

Because it was true. At least, that was what they were telling her. There had to be more conclusive tests, of course.

But how could her baby have been switched at birth with someone else's? she agonised, forcing one foot in front of the other over the last flight of stairs down from the office where they had imparted the dreaded news. And not just someone, but someone she knew. *Him!*

He had intended to summon the lift, but she had insisted on taking the stairs. After the pain of being told officially that Sean probably wasn't hers, she had needed to walk, to think, to try to recover some measure of stability.

Now, as Brant swung open the glass door to allow her into the brilliant June sunshine, she noticed the grim set of his jaw and remembered the anger he had unleashed on the two hospital officials to whom they had spoken. 'If further tests prove conclusive, you will, of course, be instructing solicitors to sort out the custody issue,' the middle-aged woman had said to Annie, as though she had been able to take it in—take anything in—right then.

'Lawyers won't be necessary.' She had barely heard Brant's succinct response, her brain still reeling from the cruel reality of it all. 'We're going to work it out for ourselves.'

Were they? At that moment, Annie could only let him conduct the interview, take control, even if she felt he was doing so against her paralysed will.

'There'll have to be an inquiry into how a thing like this could have happened,' the woman's male colleague tagged on, looking worried behind rimless steel glasses, which was when Brant's temper had seemed to snap.

'You're darn right there will! And if you don't instigate it after we've left this office, then I will!' he had threatened. 'It might be just a hiccup in the smooth running of your damned hospital, but it's turned other people's lives upside down—and someone's going to have to answer for that!'

Which was an understatement, Annie thought as the door swung closed behind Brant now. Her world hadn't just been turned upside down. Yesterday, and then last night when she hadn't been able to sleep, she had felt as though it were hanging by a thread. Now that thread had snapped and it had come crashing down around her, choking, blinding her to all but its emotional chaos.

'Come on,' she heard Brant say gently, and felt a strong hand at her elbow. 'I'll take you for a drink.'

The café to which he took her was a small bistro within walking distance of the hospital. It wasn't yet lunchtime, but the place was still humming with lively chatter.

'I can't believe this is happening,' Annie murmured, after the waiter had served them their drinks at the only small table left for two. She lifted the tall, slim glass to her lips, feeling the bitter-sweet tang of the iced grapefruit juice she had ordered zinging on her tongue, piercing through her numbness. 'I thought this sort of thing only happened to other people.'

'We are other people—to everybody else,' he remarked, his tone phlegmatic, the anger she had witnessed in him back at the hospital banked down now like carefully controlled fire.

Over the rim of her glass, Annie watched him pick up his cup of strong black coffee, her eyes reluctantly drawn to the sinewy strength of his hand. He was a stranger to her and yet she had known the caress of those strong hands, known the excitement of his crushing weight…

Rather unsteadily she returned her glass to its little slate coaster, though not before catching the disconcerting awareness in those all-seeing eyes.

'Why did you take off the way you did that Saturday morning after that party?' he was suddenly asking. 'Without saying a word to anyone?'

She looked at him quickly. Why did he have to mention that?

'Apart from ringing your boss at home and handing in your notice, no one seemed to know what happened to you—where you went.'

Toying with her glass, Annie felt her heart change rhythm. Had he asked? A slow, insidious heat stole through her veins.

She shrugged, the royal-blue top striking against the shining vitality of her hair.

'I went to France,' she told him, meeting his eyes levelly now. 'Fruit-picking. I needed a change. A break.' She had needed the time too. Time to recover her pride, and recover from the shame she had left back here in England. 'When the harvest was over, I spent time backpacking round the south of France.'

'Sounds idyllic.'

'Oh, it was!' It was easy to bluff, to pretend, now that her wounds had healed.

'Why didn't you tell me you were planning to go away?'

Because she hadn't planned it. She had simply run. 'There didn't seem to be much point.'

'Not much…' A spark of something like annoyance lit his eyes. 'After what we shared?'

She wished he hadn't reminded her, but since he had, she lifted her small chin in an almost defiant gesture and asked, 'What did we share, Brant?'

A muscle clenched in his jaw. 'You even need to ask?'

What was he saying? Why was he even making such an issue of it?

Struggling for equanimity, she said with as much non-chalance as she could muster, 'I was on the rebound. And you...' You were in love with Naomi, her brain screamed at him, because you certainly married her soon enough afterwards! Pride hurting, she cringed as she heard herself asking the question burning through her from her bitter calculations. 'Was she already pregnant when you made love to me?'

He didn't answer for a moment. How could he? she thought woundedly, watching him pick up his spoon and toy absently with the dark liquid in his cup, though he had taken it without sugar.

'Our boys were born on the same day.' He sent a casual glance upwards towards two patrons who were passing their table, his eyes returning to the spoon he let drop into its saucer. 'How do you answer that one, Annie?'

His tone might have been casual, but the intensity of his gaze impaled her, causing hot colour to flood into her cheeks.

He had been careful, of course. Unerring in his unshakeable responsibility towards her—to himself. Now it was Annie who was lost for words.

She hadn't known, when Warren had asked her to start taking the contraceptive pill, that a simple dose of antibiotics for a chest infection could render it ineffective. But it had.

Matter-of-factly, Brant stated, 'You conceived in a relationship that was falling apart.' And when she didn't answer, her lashes drooping, concealing the misery of recalling that time, he asked, 'Did the two of you ever get back together?'

'Hardly.'

'But he was aware you had his child?'

'Warren had his model. What happened to me after that wouldn't have concerned him.'

'So you didn't tell him.'

Why should I have? she thought bitterly, but didn't say it.

Quickly she lifted her glass again, took another swift draught of her juice. Already the ice was melting and it tasted less sharp, much more watery on her tongue.

'So there's no reason then for Maddox to be involved in this affair?'

Annie shook her head, replacing her glass. Across the table the eyes that studied her were like enigmatic pools.

'The man must have needed his head read,' he said softly.

Was that a compliment? Annie wondered, blushing as she considered the wild, abandoned way she had given herself to this virtual stranger sitting opposite her; wondered too just how wanton he must have considered her. But that one night of folly with him wasn't in character with the real Annie Talbot at all. Her parents had always stressed the maxim of one man—one woman—one passion. They had adhered to it themselves and, until Warren's unfaithfulness, she had thought she could easily follow in their footsteps.

She visualised them miles away in their little colonial-style house, her father quietly impatient, immobilised by a hip operation, her mother fussing over him, over-protective as usual, unaware of the shocking truth that was about to change their lives—all of their lives, she thought, the uncertainty darkening her eyes, puckering her forehead.

'What are you thinking?' Brant was setting his empty cup back on the table, eyes keen, senses sharp as a razor.

What she had been thinking during the long hours when she had been tossing and turning last night. 'I'm wondering what Mum and Dad are going to say.'

'When they find out that their grandchild's mine and not Warren Maddox's?'

For a moment his statement seemed to rock her off her axis.

'Yours and Naomi's,' she enlarged at length.

'Yes,' he said, the way his breath seemed to shudder through his lungs leaving her in no doubt of how much he must have loved his wife.

Briefly, her mind wandered back to the woman she had glimpsed once from a distance getting into Brant's car. Short, chic auburn hair and dark glasses. And that amazing height—only an inch or two shorter than Brant—which Annie, even in the four-inch heels to which he had referred earlier could never aspire to. Naomi Fox, as she had been then. Beautiful, sophisticated and intelligent—if office gossip was anything to go by—she had obviously swept Brant off his feet, then had died from a postpartum haemorrhage almost immediately after being delivered of their baby son.

Annie didn't want to think about that, or what Brant must have endured because of it. But she couldn't stop herself, in spite of everything, from considering his plight. Not only losing the woman he loved, but now learning that the child they had produced in their short marriage wasn't theirs. She wondered how he could even begin to deal with that.

And the child he was raising, this unknown child—if the hospital was to be believed—was *hers*, the child she had given birth to. The sudden crushing need to see him, know him, almost stole the breath out of her lungs.

'It isn't very easy for my mother, either.'

His mother? His surprising statement dragged her back to the present. She hadn't even considered that he might have parents. A mother. She'd imagined men like Brant merely happened. But naturally there would be other people involved, not just the two of them. Their babies. Her own parents. There would be other confused and anxious relations. Perhaps aunts and uncles. Did Brant have any brothers or sisters? Did Naomi? Suddenly, despite having shared his bed, shamefully she realised just how little she knew about him.

A mobile phone started ringing on another table, a shrill rendition of *Greensleeves,* intruding on her thoughts.

'What about Naomi's? Her parents?' she asked, irritated by the sound. 'Do they know?'

Brant turned a grim face from the neighbouring table as the ringing was answered. 'Naomi was an orphan.'

'Oh.' She hadn't expected that, imagined that anyone just a little older than herself, as Naomi must have been, might be without the parental love she had always taken for granted. But at least that was one less complication to worry about.

'There's just my mother and me,' Brant told her, unwittingly answering the question she had silently posed a few moments before.

'How is she taking it?'

'She's naturally upset. Concerned. You can't expect anything else. Ever since Jack was born, she's looked on him as her own flesh and blood. Her own grandchild. She's helped with his upbringing, looked after him when it's been difficult for me to be there. She's begged me not to let him go.'

'And you?' Annie asked, the fear and conflict in her eyes all too apparent. If he was prepared to give up the child he had raised, it would mean him having to sue for custody of Sean, because she wouldn't give him up without a fight.

'As I said yesterday, I only want what's best for both boys. Our own emotions and needs shouldn't even come into it.'

And what did he think was best? To wrench each child from the only home, the only family, it had known for two years so that it could grow up with its biological parent, regardless of how much it hurt—the child as well as its family; regardless of the emotional and psychological cost?

'I've got to pick up Sean.'

She leaped up, not caring how it looked. She only knew she had to get to her baby.

She was out in the street, gasping the polluted air. She had to get him back from Katrina's now! She needed to cuddle him. Hold him close. Know that he was safe from anything that threatened.

She almost jumped at the strong, warm hand on her shoulder.

'We'll pick him up together.' Through the roar of traffic, the blaring of car horns, Brant's voice was firm, decisive.

'No, it's all right! I can get the tube from here,' she said shakily, needing to get away from him, to hold him at bay. 'I left his car seat in my car. I can drive out and get him myself.' She was gabbling, but she couldn't help herself.

'You haven't got one. It won't be safe.'

'You're darn right it won't. You aren't in any fit state to go rushing about on tubes—and certainly not to drive anywhere,' Brant told her grimly, his self-possession emphasising Annie's own lack of composure. 'Jack's car seat's in the boot.' He took her arm, steering her out of the way of someone hurrying by. 'We'll go together,' he reiterated. 'And that's final.'

'Well, you're certainly full of surprises,' Katrina called, watching her friend coming down the garden path with Brant. A strawberry-blonde, with a thicket of short, wild curls, she had obviously seen the big car pull up and, unable to contain herself, had hurried out to greet them. Now her big blue eyes turned with reluctant appreciation towards Brant. 'You found her, then.' There was a surprising flush beneath the profusion of freckles Annie knew her friend hated.

'Yes, thank you, Katrina. Your assistance proved very fruitful.'

'My pleasure…sir,' she returned with calculated emphasis, while her gaze drifting back to Annie warned, *I hope you know what you're doing, girl!*

Quickly, Annie murmured, 'Katrina, has Sean been OK?'

Her friend's expression changed to curiosity. 'Of course. He's always OK. Why?'

Annie exhaled deeply. Of course. She was just being silly. Over-protective. She couldn't prevent breaking into a broad smile, however, when she heard the thump of tiny feet and saw the nut-brown head appear from behind Katrina.

Serious-faced, already a real little boy in his blue and red chequered shirt and dungarees, he stopped dead when he saw Brant standing there beside his mother.

'So you're Sean,' he breathed, dropping down to the child's level.

Annie's eyes darted from the man to the toddler. Was she imagining it? Or was that likeness between them as strong as the agony of her denial?

Catching the crack in Brant's voice though as he said something else to the little boy, she could only guess at the tumult of emotion he was doing his best to conceal before the toddler, suddenly shy, clutched at Katrina's denim-clad leg and disappeared behind it.

The blonde woman laughed.

'It's all right, Sean,' Annie reassured him gently, so that the little boy, deciding it was safe, popped out again, fixing Brant with curious, though steady hazel eyes.

'Kat! Fish!' the child exclaimed proudly. 'Kat! Fish!'

'Catfish?' The man's smile was indulgent, softening the severity of his features. From her vantage point Annie noticed how wide his shoulders were beneath the soft grey polo shirt, how the fabric of his chinos pulled tautly across his thighs.

'Kat-fish,' the two-year-old announced, rather impatiently this time, and in spite of the chaos inside her, Annie couldn't keep from smiling when she realised what he meant.

'Katrina's embroidered an octopus on his new bib.' It was bright yellow on its pale blue background, with disjointed eyes and tentacles. Her friend was always doing things like that. She managed to laugh. 'It's gross, Kat!'

'No, it isn't.' Katrina grinned. 'It's a friendly little octopus.' She pretended to be one, sending Sean shrieking down the passageway. 'It's only big fish that gobble you up and then spit you out again. Isn't that right, Seanie?'

It was child's play, but Annie felt the keen glance Brant sliced her as he got to his feet. Mortified, she caught her breath. They both knew what Katrina meant.

They were silent as Brant drove them back to the flat. Sean had fallen asleep in the back of the car in the little seat Brant had produced from the boot.

'Sorry about Katrina. She can be a bit direct sometimes.' She felt she needed to say something because he was just sitting there steering the powerful saloon. Hard lines carved what she had always thought was a rather cruel mouth.

'What did you tell her about us?' He was pulling up at a zebra crossing to let a middle-aged woman step on. She beamed at him and he responded with a distracted nod of his head. 'Everything down to the last graphic detail?'

'Of course not!' she snapped, heated colour stealing into her cheeks. 'She guessed. I think everyone did.'

'That I bedded a freshly betrayed bride. And then dumped her just as Maddox did.'

No, not as Warren did, she thought as he put the car into motion again. Because Brant Cadman had made her no promises. Offered her nothing but one crazy, glorious night. She'd known the dangerous game she was playing when she had let him take her up to his room; known what she was doing, even though she had had just a little too much to drink that night, too much for her at any rate. It had been he who had suggested calling a halt to their caresses. He who had tried to tell her he didn't believe in fooling around with women on the rebound, when she had so foolishly begged him not to go.

Her cheeks burned now with the shame of it and way down inside she felt the fierce pang of unwelcome desire undermined by the cutting pain of rejection.

'Katrina's my friend,' she told him, ridiculously emotional. 'She was only looking out for my interests.' Suddenly she needed some spur, a point of antagonism to stab at the whole agonising trauma of the day. 'I suppose in a minute you'll be telling me you objected to her calling my boy ''Seanie''!' she tossed at him, with an emphasis on the 'my boy' that hit its mark if that tightening muscle in his jaw was anything to go by.

She heard him catch his breath and, after a moment, felt him glance her way.

'Come on,' he said. 'We're both wound up. This has been an ordeal for both of us. Let's not quarrel to add to it. It will all be sorted out a lot more painlessly if we remain civil.'

She nodded, saying nothing. But at least that seemed to ease some of the tension between them.

Outside her flat, she was first out of the car, reaching into the back to try and free Sean from the unfamiliar seat.

'Here, let me,' Brant advised.

Leaning across the seat, he had released him in a second. Head lolling to one side, Sean was still sleeping soundly.

'May I?' Brant whispered.

Annie swallowed, nodded. Well he had to some time, didn't he?

As he picked up the sleeping child, his features were marked with raw emotion and Annie felt the almost painful constriction of her throat.

What was he thinking, looking for, as those dark, searching eyes roamed over the infant? Some resemblance to the woman he'd loved? Had he already wondered, just as she had, if that distinctive little nose could be his? That the sun-streaked, tawny hair could be a feature of his wife's and not hers—hers and Warren's—as he could easily have supposed?

Fear rose in her again, the feeling that she was in danger of losing the only thing that really mattered to her—her baby—and immediately they were inside the flat she retrieved him from Brant.

When he was tucked up in bed for his afternoon nap she fed Bouncer, who was mewing around her ankles in the kitchen, and went back to join Brant in the sitting room.

He was looking at her paintings, particularly the miniature of a mistle thrush she was still working on. There were landscapes too. A sunset over a shadowy headland and a steam train, its plume of blue smoke like a heralding flag above the cutting of a distant hill.

'These are good. They're very good,' he complimented.

At any other time she would have derived great pleasure from his saying so. Now, though, in view of everything, all she felt was a mild satisfaction that her labours were appreciated.

'Thank you,' she said.

'We're going to have to arrange for you to see Jack.' He had straightened again, dominating the small room with his sheer presence. 'Maybe tomorrow I can—'

'No!' Her panicked response put a query in his eyes. Hers were darkened almost to black. 'I can't—yet.' She could feel herself trembling. Even her voice shook. 'I'm not ready,' she uttered, trying to make him understand.

She hankered after knowing what her birth child—if he was her child—was like. She also knew any meeting with him would be all too traumatic at present.

Suddenly she looked very pale and weary, a small, vulnerable figure in her clinging top and cropped trousers, shoulders slumping with emotional fatigue.

A couple of strides brought him over to her and somehow, she didn't quite know how, she was standing in the circle of his arms with her cheek against the hard, warm wall of his chest.

In the silence of the room, she could hear the heavy rhythm of his heart, then from the kitchen the swift, dull clack of the cat-flap.

She raised her head, lifting her face to his, the need in those green-gold eyes meeting an answering need in Annie.

His lips were gentle on hers, a light, tentative touch meant only to console, an offer of solace from one troubled human being to another.

Annie groaned from deep in her throat, and, unable to stop herself, let her arms slide up around his neck.

His breathing quickened in response, and he caught her to him, his arms tightening around her yielding softness, drawing her hard against him.

His kiss had deepened into something more sensual and demanding, and Annie returned it with a fervour she hadn't known she was still capable of, needing his strength, to be engulfed by the powerful aura of his sexuality and his hard-edged masculinity that was suddenly as familiar to her as her own name.

She wasn't sure at what point she felt him withdraw. She only knew he had and she uttered a small protest when he unclasped her hands from behind his head and dragged them down, leaving her silently pleading, cast adrift, humiliated.

'No, Annie. This will just complicate things,' he stressed, but the raw intensity in his voice and his laboured breathing assured her that he was just as affected as she was. 'I think it would be best if I left you for the time being. We're both frayed by what has happened. Today hasn't been easy—for either of us, but I think particularly for you. You need time to adjust to things. We both do. May I?' He was indicating Sean's bedroom door.

How could she stop him? she wondered achingly.

When she nodded he pushed the door quietly open, and just stood there in the doorway, gazing across at the sleeping infant.

After a few moments he moved back out again, and gently closed the door.

'I'll be in touch,' he told her, his voice thick with restrained emotion. 'In the meantime I think you should telephone your parents. They're really going to have to know.'

When he had gone, Annie sank down into a chair.

How could she? she thought, ashamed of the way she had behaved with him. How could she have been so stupid? Hadn't she learned by now that caresses and tender kisses meant very little to a man? That they could demonstrate one thing and mean entirely another? Hadn't she grasped that yet? Not only with him, but before with Warren, with every man she'd given more than a passing glance to?

It was her behaviour with Brant that she least wanted to remember. But her actions today had only served to bring it all back.

She had been ensnared from the moment she had first laid eyes on Brant Cadman, a reluctant victim of his dark, enslaving sexuality. She had denied it, of course, betrothed as she was to another man. But the fact that he had noticed her, too, had been doubly disturbing.

She had been working in the art and design department of Cadman Sport for just a few weeks when she had met Warren Maddox. A young, thrusting executive in the sales and marketing side of the company that came under the massive umbrella of Cadman Leisure, Warren had swept Annie off her feet. With her parents embarking on their dream to emigrate to New Zealand, change and excitement seemed to encompass them all when, within a month of their departure, Warren had asked her to marry him and they had become engaged.

He was never madly passionate, but he was kind and caring—or so she had thought. He was also clever, perhaps a little calculating where his clients were concerned, and he was humorous. Sometimes a bit too flippant, Annie had felt occasionally, but that had merely seemed to add to making him fun to be with.

It was at a seminar they had both attended in Birmingham that she had seen Brant for the first time.

'I've got to get to talk to him,' Warren told her after the talks were over, and skittered across the room, pulling Annie in tow, determined as he was to get himself noticed by Brant Cadman.

Clean-cut, impeccably dressed in a tailored dark suit and tie, his hard-headed brilliance and formidable authority was a mixture that would have arrested attention even without the smoky sexuality that transcended all these other attributes. He looked fierce, Annie recalled. Fierce and terrifyingly attractive and he scared her half to death. And she'd never been so drawn to any man in her life!

She couldn't even remember what had been said. Only the way Brant looked at her while he was talking to them both, indulging them, she decided, because Warren's eagerness to ingratiate himself with the big boss was embarrassingly obvious. But she felt the man's gaze on her afterwards wherever she was in the room, discreet yet unmistakably appraising. She wasn't even sure she liked him, but she was shockingly aroused by his interest nevertheless. That shamed and disturbed her, because she had thought herself head over heels in love with Warren. Brant, too, was obviously involved with someone else—it was afterwards, outside the hotel, that she saw his chic, tall companion climbing into his car. Someone—she couldn't remember who now—told her the woman's name. Naomi Fox. It suited her, Annie thought, telling herself she had imagined those glances from him. Telling herself that her reaction to them was only from the mere excitement of being noticed by a man way out of her league, that she was engaged to be married, eager to settle down and be happy.

Yet alone in bed that night, trying to concentrate on her fiancé and her forthcoming wedding, it was Brant's dark features that kept rising before her eyes and which troubled her dreams so that she awoke agitated and feverish and disliking him even more.

It wore off, of course. The reality of a looming wedding with all its attendant concerns kept her occupied and focused on her main aim in life—that of becoming Mrs Warren Maddox. But two weeks before the due date he told her that he couldn't go through with it; that he had met someone else and that he was sorry, but he was calling it off.

Annie was devastated. Hurt and shell-shocked, with everyone at Cadman's aware that they had split up, it was trial enough seeing Warren in the office when he wasn't off finding potential clients. But having to attend that party two weeks later to celebrate the opening of a new hotel and sports complex was the most humiliating of all.

Her boss insisted she go and she didn't want to let him down. Besides, she thought, even if she was feeble enough to ring in sick, everyone would guess the reason why. Everyone, that was, who made up not only the art and design department, but Sales and Marketing too. Which meant that Warren would be going and, as partners were invited, most certainly his new girlfriend, and there was no way, she decided, that she would give either of them the satisfaction of seeing her buckle, let them—let anyone—guess at the agonies she was suffering from his cruel betrayal. What she didn't anticipate, however, was that Brant Cadman would be attending too, that he'd be staying at the hotel that night.

Glass in hand, a daringly low-cut black dress emphasising her slim figure, she was chatting rather over-brightly to Katrina and her boss, trying to look cheerful, pretending that the sight of her ex-fiancé and his new blonde bombshell, wrapped up in each other not six feet away, didn't matter to her at all, when she saw him standing, tall and erect, at the bar.

He had been talking to various people until then, employees and clients alike, desperate to make his acquaintance. But now he was alone, and he was looking straight at her.

Annie's heart seemed to stop and then start again, beating slightly faster than before. She lifted her chin in a somewhat challenging gesture, not sure how to respond to his blatant interest.

He smiled then, a lazy, sensuous, cognizant smile that would have shattered any woman's immunity.

She smiled back.

'Wow!' she heard Katrina exclaim.

Emboldened by a couple of glasses of wine, Annie excused herself from her little group and, with what she considered afterwards could only have been subconscious intent, moved over to the bar. At the time it felt as though those beautiful eyes alone were drawing her to him.

'Hello,' was all he said, but his deep voice oozed a lethal charm that didn't altogether fool her. Behind the smooth urbanity was an even more lethal brain.

She responded, flashed him a brilliant smile.

'What happened to your...friend?' He didn't look in Warren's direction, but he had to be aware of the situation. Instead his glance touched on the ringless finger curled around her wine glass.

'Friends fall out.'

'And lovers?'

She took a breath, swallowed. God! What was she doing? She stole a covert glance in Warren's direction. He was looking at her—at them both, displaying a shock that matched Katrina's moments before when she had realised where her friend was headed. She flashed Brant another smile, and in a voice as silvery as the threads running through her clinging black dress, murmured, 'And you, Mr Cadman...'

'Brant.'

'Are you...involved?'

He seemed to consider her question, before lifting his hands. They were long and well-tapered. 'I'm as you see me. I'm not, however, quite so sure about you.'

'What do you mean by that?'

His eyes strayed to Warren and the blonde, who were now dancing to a slow, sultry blues number.

'She's welcome to him.' She tried desperately for nonchalance, her lashes veiling the dark anguish in her eyes. 'She'll find out he's a louse.'

'And you think I'm not?'

She lifted her chin, her lips a scarlet invitation to him, though she was dying inside. 'Are you?'

'Do you know what I think?' he said.

'What?'

He reached to take the glass out of her hand, put it on the bar.

'I think you've had too much to drink.'

'No, I haven't.' In truth, she had had barely two glasses, but on an empty stomach, having eaten very frugally for days because of her misery and then her apprehension over having to facing Warren with Caroline, it had obviously been too much.

'OK, so you haven't,' he accepted, humouring her. 'So tell me about Annie Talbot.'

She had been surprised that he remembered her name. When Warren had introduced her to him at that seminar two months before, he had been distracted by someone leaning over to say something to him, and she'd thought he hadn't even heard. But obviously the man was as astute as he was dangerous, she thought with an unexpected little shiver, wondering why her brain should conjure up such a profound adjective in connection with him.

Wrinkling her nose, however, she murmured, 'Far too boring. I'd rather talk about you.'

'Would you?' He made it sound like a reprimand so that at first she thought he wasn't going to comply. But then he shrugged and said, 'I'm thirty-two years old. Six feet two inches tall. Difficult to live with and have been chastised for more than just having a bad temper in my time. I also never make a habit of seducing young women on the re-bound.'

'Very commendable,' Annie purred. Her legs felt like two tubs of lead and her face was aching from the need to keep on smiling.

'Shall we dance?' he suggested, and when she nodded led her towards the small polished circle where Warren and his lovely model swayed with eyes only for each other.

'What would you like me to do?' Brant enquired as he took Annie in his arms. 'Punch him on the nose?'

Was her misery that obvious? she thought, and made a special effort to laugh.

'Now, why would I want that?' she breathed, her devil-may-care attitude bringing her hands across the wide sweep of his shoulders. 'It really isn't that important,' she said, then gasped as his arm tightened like a steel bar against the small of her back, drawing her against his hard body.

She trembled in his arms and her mouth went dry. She felt slightly giddy from the heady musk of his cologne. Suddenly she realised what a dangerous game she was playing, that she was way, way out of her league. What did it matter though, she thought, if she could keep everyone from guessing how she was really feeling? Salve her pride and her dignity and her self-respect?

But the effort of pretending she didn't care was wearing her out. Her head was aching now and her energy seemed to have deserted her. Also, behind them, Warren and the model were entwined in an intimate clinch, mouths devouring each other in a way that was overtly sexual.

Annie tried not to notice, but she couldn't avoid it. Almost inaudibly she groaned, dipped her head, and felt the soft wool of Brant's jacket against her forehead.

It was a far too intimate action, but one she could no more have avoided making than waking in the morning. As she swayed, she heard Brant say gently, 'Come on.'

She hadn't intended to wind up in his room. Any more than he, she felt, had intended they should wind up in bed. Not together anyway. He had simply been intending she should rest, she was certain, when he had carried her, like a rag doll, into his bedroom and laid her down on the cool, sensuous cotton of the duvet. Her head burned and she was racked by a tense excitement she had never known before. She watched him discard his jacket and tie before he came back and sat down beside her, asked if she was all right.

It was that one light kiss that had done it, that gentle probing of her lips before he made to move away that had her clutching at his shirt like a drowning man to a piece of driftwood. 'Stay with me,' foolishly she had murmured.

By the time she had realised the implications of what she was saying—doing—she was in the grip of a subjugating passion she had no will or desire to control. She had used him to blot out her misery, and didn't expect after one mindblowing climax in Brant's bed that Warren Maddox would blur into insignificance, that in the morning her overriding emotion would be raw shame. Because how strong must her feelings for her fiancé have been in the first place, she wondered, if she could be reduced to such a wanton, sobbing creature, craving fulfilment by a man she'd merely seduced while on the rebound?

Rising before he was even awake, she raced home to pack, rang her boss to quit her job, then fled to Provence and anonymity.

It was when she had returned from France two months later that Katrina had told her Brant was married. Annie hadn't seen him again until he had turned up at the flat the previous afternoon. Warren, as far as she had been aware, had moved in with his precious model. And, of course, when she had returned to England she had been in the early stages of pregnancy with Sean.

Brant had driven the pain of Warren's betrayal away, only to replace it with a shaming humiliation. And with what skill and expertise! she thought now, trying not to dwell too deeply on the devastating few hours she had spent in his arms, telling herself again that she would be a fool to throw herself back into them, no matter how dangerously her hormones reacted to him. He had simply taken what she had had to offer at the time and then gone off and married Naomi Fox, and she had no one to blame but herself.

But one thing he wasn't going to do was take Sean away! she determined, forcing herself up out of the chair and throwing herself into unnecessary household chores to try and keep her raging anxieties at bay.

And later, as soon as it was a respectable time to do so, unable to wait a minute longer, she did as he had advised, picked up the phone and tapped out the international dialling code for New Zealand.

CHAPTER THREE

ANNIE tried to concentrate on the little miniature painting, but nothing was working. Neither her brain, nor her fingers, nor her brush. Even the paint she was using for her foreground on the smooth translucent surface had blended with her horizon to create an unwanted, indistinct blur.

Like her life, Annie thought. Or at least how it had become since Brant had turned up there five days ago, threatening everything she valued, loved.

He was coming round at twelve to take her back to his home so that she could meet the little boy the hospital claimed was hers.

Annie's hands trembled as she discarded the painting she had started earlier in the hope of losing herself in something useful, because as much as she was longing for this meeting, now that the time was almost upon her she was afraid, too.

How would she react when she came face to face with the toddler? This child to whom she was supposed to have given birth? Would she feel any maternal bond? Anything? Would she recognise him? Would there be some instinctive feeling in him towards her? And if there was, what would she do then? Because she couldn't—wouldn't—give up Sean.

'He's ours, Annie. Of course he is!' She remembered Jane Talbot's words coming shrilly across miles of ocean the evening she had rung her parents. 'It doesn't matter how many tests they say they have to do. They'll only show up that he's ours. Oh, my goodness! I want to come over,' the woman had raced on. 'I wish I could come right away, but I can't leave your father. He needs me too much at the moment. Whatever am I going to do?'

Annie had been grateful that she had spoken to her father first; that he had been nearest the phone to pick it up when she had rung, because she hadn't been able to stop herself breaking down, let alone cope with her mother's hysterics as well. Though he had been naturally shocked and unhappy when she had told him that the grandson they adored might not be their grandson at all, Simon Talbot had taken it as he took everything life threw at him, good or bad. In his quiet, rational and unruffled way.

'Annie. Annie,' he'd soothed, hiding his own distress in an attempt to console his daughter. 'This man Cadman and his wife…they're going to feel the same way as you do. Of course they are. They won't want to give up the child they've been bringing up as their own. They might want visitation rights to what might be their natural child—just as you might—but they—'

'No, Dad. You don't understand.' She hadn't made it clear, she had realised then. 'Brant's lost his wife. Therefore he's got even more reason to want to take my baby away—because he's part of her. Part of what he's lost. Don't you see…?'

From the silence that came across the miles, Annie had realised that he did. She could visualize his dear, familiar face, those character lines deepening beneath the black and grey peppered hair, his lean frame partially immobilised as he lounged, frustrated at having to relinquish his golf and his sailing, but most of all his staunch independence, to the ministrations of his easily overwrought wife.

'If he's a reasonable man, he wouldn't hurt you like that, Annie. He'll see it your way as well.'

But would he? Annie thought now, remembering her father's words, as well as how exhausted she had been after she had come off the phone.

Traumatised as she had been herself, trying to console her mother had drained her, along with trying to convince Jane Talbot that she couldn't possibly think about leaving her husband, so she shouldn't worry. Annie had Katrina, didn't she, who was a good friend. So she wasn't entirely alone.

Tidying her paints, and pushing back her magnifier on the anglepoise lamp, she took the brush in its jar out to the kitchen sink, rinsing them both under the tap. She felt awful for thinking it, but much as she needed a shoulder to lean on, she was aware of a measure of relief that her mother couldn't come. She didn't think she could have stood Jane Talbot's fussing on top of everything else.

It had been agreed that Annie would meet Jack before introducing Sean to any other members of Brant's household. It being Saturday, Katrina had taken him off to the bouncy castle in the local park, where Annie always took him as a special treat.

'I don't have to tell you to be careful, do I?' her friend had warned her knowingly as Annie was gathering up Sean's little cap and cuddly lion for him to take. 'All that stupendous arrogance and dynamism! Unless you're less vulnerable than you were—what was it? Three years ago?'

'Not quite,' Annie had corrected. 'And it isn't what you're imagining, Katrina.' Unable to keep it to herself any longer, she had told her friend the truth.

The woman had been shocked, then sympathetic, her arms going around Annie in such a caring hug she'd felt tears bite behind her eyes.

'Ten times *more* vulnerable,' the woman had cautioned, so that now as she went into the bathroom, turned on the shower, Annie felt an ominous little shiver run along her spine.

Forty minutes later, the purr of a car engine had her rushing to the bedroom window. She reached it just in time to see Brant stepping out of the Mercedes in the tree-lined street.

Her gaze locked on him, following his long, lithe physique, impeccably encased in a dark business suit, until his glance up at the window made her pull away, wondering if he had noticed her reluctant interest.

'Are you ready?' At the door, his eyes made a swift survey of her mock-suede lilac jacket and the low-slung trousers she had teamed with a cream silk camisole.

She nodded, and saw his brow furrow as he studied her pale, tense features.

'How do you feel?'

Annie inhaled deeply. 'Terrified,' she admitted.

His mouth pulled down on one side. 'Is that why you pretended not to see me just now? Are you terrified of me, too?'

She was. Of those energies and that forceful determination that had brought him from a working-class background to millionaire status in just a few short years, if what she had heard about him was right. Of his charisma and charm and that intensely masculine attraction that had once swept the very ground from under her, and still had the power to do it again if she let it. But above all, of what he might come to represent.

'Of course not,' she lied, and, unable to stand the waiting any longer, murmured, 'Can we go?'

His home was a huge Georgian house in one of the most sought-after suburbs of the city. A place that intimidated her on her first impression with its august formality, with its myriad windows that looked out on to extensive, perfectly maintained grounds.

'Mother lived in Shropshire—in a busy little town she didn't really want to leave—and where we both came from originally,' he explained as they got out of the car, which was as much as he was going to tell her then, she realised, about his more humble beginnings. 'When...Jack came on the scene, she moved down here to help out so that Jack wouldn't be with total strangers whenever I went away. And then, so it doesn't get too much for her, we have Elise.'

Annie glanced up at him, curious, as he was locking the car, but he didn't enlarge.

Now, as she entered the formal drawing room with the tall man at her side, she felt the unsettling interest of the slim, subtly-blonde woman who was moving towards them with an elegance befitting her surroundings, and guessed that this could only be Brant's mother.

'I see what you mean,' was the woman's first remark with a startled glance up at Brant, so that Annie, catching his almost indiscernible nod, wondered what he had been saying about her.

'I'm sorry.' Her hostess smiled and, quickly recovering herself, extended a hand, her manners as polished as her pale-tipped fingers. 'I'm Felicity Cadman, and you're Annie, aren't you? The other devastated party in all this. You must feel dreadful, my dear—as in limbo as we all are. I don't know about Brant, but for me, it hasn't really sunk in.'

'Nor for me,' Annie murmured, able, through her own chaotic emotions, to sympathise with Brant's mother.

She could feel the woman's quiet assessment of her, discreet yet curious glances that conveyed what she must have been thinking since Annie had walked in. *Is this really the mother of the grandson I've helped raise?*

'I take it Jack's in the nursery?'

Of course. They would have a nursery, Annie thought as Brant's mother nodded. Living in such refinement, if Sean really were his, his and Naomi's, then wouldn't he want to make sure his son was part of it?

Everything inside her rebelled against such thinking as Brant started to lead her away, just as the phone pinged on a table close by, doing nothing for her edginess and her racing heart.

Brant snatched it up from the mirror-polished surface, grunted something about being tied up to whoever was on the line. But they must have told him it was urgent, because after his curt, 'Excuse me,' to Annie, he turned away, to take the call.

Probably some vital decision that needed his sanction, she thought, staring at the sculpted white marble of the fire sur- round, an exquisitely glazed vase sitting on top, aware of his deep voice ushering orders with that authority that made him a force to be reckoned with, yet respected and admired too, she remembered, among his competitors and his em- ployees.

Conscious of Felicity watching her, Annie dragged her gaze away from the vase.

'It's beautiful,' she uttered with an awkward smile and for something to say, only fully alive to her queasy antici- pation and the impatience in the deep voice on the other side of the room.

'Yes.' Brant's mother inhaled sharply. This whole situa- tion was a strain for her also. 'Yes, it was my…daughter- in-law's choice.'

Tensely, Annie nodded, noting the slight hesitancy in the woman's voice. As though it still hurt to speak about Brant's wife. As though she preferred not to in his presence.

And this room, Annie wondered, with its high, ornate ceiling, its silvery brocades and pale Georgian hues, had this been Naomi's choice too? Or had she and Brant chosen things together like any normal couple setting up home for the first time? In unison. In harmony. In love.

'It hasn't been easy for my son,' that cultured female voice beside her commented, and then more softly, 'what with…losing Jack's mother so…' She didn't finish, only added, 'And now this.'

And me. Does anyone think it's easy for me? Annie won- dered, her features drawn tight with anguish. She didn't even realise how militant she looked until she heard Felicity's request.

'You will consider Jack, won't you?' Beneath the elegant poise, her eyes—the only thing about her that resembled

Brant—seemed to be begging, *Please don't take my grand-son away!* 'This is the only home—only family—he's known, as it will have been for your little boy. We have to consider them. We can't pull their worlds apart, as we would if we decided to switch them back.'

'There's no question of my wanting to switch them back, or of my ever giving Sean up,' Annie stated, adamantly, just as Brant came off the phone.

'Ready?' he enquired, his arm extended.

There was a calculating watchfulness about him, she sensed, noting the contrasting, fleeting smile he directed at his mother. Which said what? she wondered as he led her through the imposing hallway, up to the second storey. That he would do what he had to, what was necessary? But surely he would feel the same way about Jack as she felt about Sean?

Her heart was pounding like a steam-hammer when he opened the door to what was obviously the nursery, with its eggshell-blue paintwork and brightly patterned walls, and the toys scattered over the floor. Across the room, a win-dow-seat offered a view of the billiard-table lawns, of high, professionally cultivated hedges.

'Monsieur Cadman...' Someone was coming out of an adjoining room. 'You want to see Jack. He has just finished lunch. He wash his own face. He is a big boy now.' Blonde, full-busted and naturally pretty, she had an accent as allur-ing as the long, swishing hair, Annie noted, as the French girl laughed up at Brant, and spared Annie no more than a passing glance before giving her attention to her employer again with an intensity that was painful to watch. 'Do you want me to stay, *monsieur*?'

'No, I'll call you, Elise.'

'*Oui, monsieur.*' The girl almost bobbed at him before leaving the room.

Somewhere in her subconscious, Annie wondered if the girl's transparent adulation amused him, or even if he'd considered doing anything about it, because Elise certainly wanted him to, but at that moment she was too distracted to care. All her attention was on the toddler who, at the sound of his father's voice, had come tottering out of the bathroom. In a tiny red shirt and miniature combat trousers, he was now flinging his arms around Brant's long, immaculately clad leg.

'Hey, hey, Jack!' With playful ease, Brant swung him up into the air, making the boy squeal in delight before setting him down on his feet again. 'Jack, I want you to meet Annie,' he said softly, clasping the infant's little hand in his. 'Annie, this is Jack.'

Moved beyond her wildest imagination, Annie could only stand there for a moment, aware of Brant's gaze lancing across her face, aware as she crouched down to say, 'Hello,' of those shrewd eyes still watching her, missing nothing. Not the way she stared, transfixed, at the little mop of thick, dark hair falling forward just as hers did, or those deep brown eyes that gazed curiously back at her, like wide, dark mirrors of her own. His face was rounder than Sean's, still in the final stages of babyhood, but unlike Sean, there was no shyness here, just a broad, toothy smile that tugged at Annie's heart, tugged at everything in her that was maternal.

'He looks like me,' she whispered in a voice thickened by emotion. Was this the child she had carried all those long months in her womb? Put to her breast before those almost immediate problems that had denied her the chance to go on suckling her own child? Or had it been Naomi Cadman's child by then? 'He looks just like me.'

Through misty eyes she watched Jack toddle over to the window-seat, grab a colouring book that had been lying there and teeter unsteadily back with it dangling unceremoniously from his little hand.

'Steady!' Brant warned, just before the two-year-old made it safely back to Annie, waving the book demandingly in front of her.

''Ow!' he declared proudly as she steadied it to look at the cow he had coloured in with a bright purple pencil, with no respect at all for its carefully drawn edges.

'It's my favourite colour,' she breathed on a choked, disbelieving note, while Jack, oblivious to the havoc he was creating in her, threw the book down and stamped on it hard.

'Een face!' he announced, tilting his little chin up for Annie to inspect. As he probably did, she thought, for his nanny, or his grandmother or whoever happened to be looking after him—just as she had taught Sean to do. There was what looked like a scrap of boiled egg yolk clinging to one downy eyebrow.

'You missed a bit,' she murmured huskily, picking it off. Suddenly, overwhelmed, she reached out and caught him to her, her sobbed emotion muffled by the scented softness of his hair.

Finding himself bear-hugged by a total stranger, Jack began to wail.

'It's OK, Jack.' As Annie reluctantly released him, gently Brant picked him up. She felt the brush of his sleeve against hers, smelled that familiar scent of him before he towered over her again. 'She's a nice lady. She wouldn't hurt you,' she heard him reassuring the infant in his deep, soothing voice.

Perched safely on his father's arm, the toddler looked bravely down at Annie now.

''Ice lady,' he cooed with that heart-wrenching, toothy smile.

'Well, not exactly, son,' Brant responded, and despite the emotion-charged mood of the moment, as he glanced down at her, she saw the half-amused curl to his lips.

From that subtle remark and the intensity of those glittering irises she knew he had to be remembering that wild night nearly three years ago, when she had so shamelessly given herself to him. He must have thought her the hottest thing ever to come out of Cadman Sport, she decided, mortified, and from the way those green-gold eyes narrowed—took in the heated colour that stained her cheeks—he knew that she was remembering it too.

He was, however, moving across to open the nursery door, calling out to Elise, who materialised on demand. As everyone would, Annie couldn't help thinking. His household staff. Waiters. His women…

'Take Jack out into the sunshine,' he advised the girl, who, after a rather searching look at Annie, promptly obeyed.

'Why didn't you let him stay?' Annie challenged as he closed the door.

'Because we need to talk. Alone.' He was stooping to pick up one or two toys, looking every bit the seasoned father as he dropped them into a bright plastic crate obviously kept for the purpose. But then he straightened and stood looking across at her, his features taut and grim.

'There isn't any doubt, is there?' he said. 'We can have the recommended DNA tests done, but in the end they'll just be a formality. It goes without saying, doesn't it? You've got my son. I've got yours.'

Too affected by the whole situation, Annie couldn't speak. She swallowed, tried again and failed.

'What I propose,' he went on calmly, betraying no sign of the emotions that were ravaging Annie, 'is that you and Sean move in here with me for a transitional period for me to get to know my son. For you to get to know yours. For the boys, in particular, to get to know who we are before any further decisions can be made.'

'Move in with you…here?' She thought of the magnificent rooms they had passed, his way of life with its servants and its smooth-running formality. No wonder he wanted to remove Sean from her modest little flat!

'Oh, don't worry,' he advised, reading the thought that had tumbled as quickly on top of all the others. 'I'm not looking for a mistress, if that's what you're wondering.'

So that told her, she thought, feeling she had just been put in her place.

'And then what?' she queried, fear coiling in her stomach. Would he expect her to give up Sean after this…transitional period? Could he give up Jack? How could anyone decide? And what about herself? she wondered. How would she handle living under the same roof as Brant Cadman, who was not only a threat to everything she treasured, but a threat to her equilibrium as well?

'Let's cross that bridge when we come to it,' he advised. He was moving over to the phone, which was fixed on the wall, out of reach of tiny hands. Picking it up, he said, 'I'll arrange for someone to have your things brought over.' Already he had started pressing buttons.

'What? Now? Today?' Annie gulped as he spoke into the mouthpiece.

'Have you any objection?'

It didn't matter whether she had or not. Nor did he expect any, she thought as he started issuing instructions to a member of staff.

'I think the sooner the better,' he told her. 'Don't you?'

And that was it, Annie realised, only able to agree. After all, what he was suggesting did make some sort of sense.

'Bloomin' Henry! That's quick!' Katrina expressed after she had returned Sean to the flat that afternoon and Annie told her of her plans. Now, sipping coffee in Annie's small kitchen, concern showed under the woman's abundant freckles. 'You do know what you're doing, do you?'

'No.' Annie grimaced, making light of her own misgivings as she sorted out cans of cat food for Katrina, who had happily agreed to look after Bouncer. The cat was noisily lapping milk, oblivious to Sean's rather heavy-handed stroking and Brant's handyman-chauffeur transferring some of their belongings out to the waiting Range Rover. 'It's just a short-term arrangement to help the boys. There isn't any more to it than that, believe me.'

'Isn't there?' Katrina was surveying her suspiciously, but Annie avoided her eyes. She felt hurt, confused and angry about the whole infernal mix-up without her friend reading more into it than there actually was. 'You're moving in with a man who's pretty damn near irresistible, and you're telling me you're not the teeniest bit affected by it?'

'I didn't think you'd noticed,' Annie parried with a half-smile in an attempt to deflect her friend's curiosity from her own worries.

'Oh, I'd noticed all right—which is why I'm so concerned.'

Which was sweet of her, Annie thought, and told her so, and was grateful that Katrina knew when to let a subject drop.

The room Annie had been given was close to the nursery and the boys' bedrooms, but was no less formal than the rest of the house. Spacious, with its own equally spacious *en-suite* bathroom, no expense had been spared on the luxurious furnishings and the fabrics that hung against the long windows, over and around the huge double bed.

Her battered old suitcase looked incongruous standing, emptied, against the immaculate wardrobe, and she lifted it out of sight, putting it into a cupboard with her box of art materials, though when she ever hoped to finish another painting feeling the way she did, she couldn't imagine.

Now, with Brant out of the house, his mother organising dinner and the rather uncommunicative Elise Dubois keeping an eye on the two boys in the nursery, Annie wandered down into the garden, glad of some time to herself.

The grounds breathed a formality as intimidating as the rest of the house. Everything was landscaped, the flower borders weed-free, not a shrub nor blade of grass out of place. Perfect, sterile and quite soulless, Annie decided, coming to a recess in the immaculately clipped hedge of cypress trees hemming the path.

She would have liked to sit down on the ornate iron seat, but the cast-bronze statue of a woman on a stone pedestal presiding over it seemed to disapprove and so she remained on her feet, viewing the sculpture with the same mixed feelings she had for the rest of the place.

'So this is where you're hiding.'

The familiar deep voice had her swinging round, and started her heart thumping. She hadn't seen him since he had left her with his handyman to bring her things back earlier, telling her he had a business meeting in town.

'I wasn't hiding,' she countered, weakening from the sheer impact of his dark virility. 'I was just taking advantage of a few moments' solitude.'

'And now I've robbed you of them.'

'Yes,' she uttered, deriving some satisfaction in making him feel unwelcome. Perhaps it was this house, she thought. Or him. Or both.

'And you'd prefer it if I went away again.' An uncertain note in his voice made him seem a little unsure and she rather liked the idea of seeing him at a disadvantage.

'I'm sure you'll do whatever you like.'

'In other words you're trying to tell me I like to have all my own way?'

'Don't you?' she accused with a fleeting, humourless smile. After all, since he had stampeded into her life less than a week ago with that devastating declaration about Sean, he had seemed to take every decision away from her, even down to her coming here.

'I suppose I could be considered guilty of that,' he conceded with a contemplative smile. 'I'm afraid it's a trait I've been told I've possessed since childhood.'

'Then it's time someone cured you of it.' She hadn't realised she had expressed her thoughts until they were out.

'And are you proposing to be that someone, Annie?'

Mouth twitching at the corners, he allowed his gaze to roam over the casual top and trousers she had substituted for her lilac suit earlier, and she felt herself blushing to the roots of her hair.

'I'm not proposing anything,' she stated flatly.

Now he had her at a disadvantage and she could see he was relishing it. Which just served her right, she thought, for imagining she could tamper with that daunting self-confidence in the first place!

Agitated, she cast an unconscious glance up at the disapproving bronze.

'She's pretty magnificent,' she breathed for something to say. *Like these gardens. Like the house. Like you!*

He sent a cursory glance towards the statute. 'Yes,' he said heavily. 'She is.'

'Where did you get her?'

He seemed to hesitate before answering, but then said, 'She was Naomi's choice. When we bought this house, the gardens were in need of a lot of attention. She organised most of it. She bought this while we were honeymooning in Italy. But then most of her ideas for the garden came from Paris or Rome.' The sun streaked fire through his hair as he inclined his head, surveying the figure more intently now. 'I always thought it represented everything she was.'

Yes, tall and chic and elegant, Annie thought, snatching a stealthy glance up at him. A lean hunger seemed to tauten the hard cast of his features, making her wonder how much he still grieved for the woman to whom he had been married for less than a year. She couldn't forget how utterly striking the two of them had looked together, so tall and impressive—so that she had felt as small as she did now beside him and his wife's beautiful statue—insignificant in comparison.

'It seems rather ironic my being here, doesn't it?' she commented, shivering as a chilly breeze moved along the line of cypress trees, her words prompted by a cold, irrational hurt. After all, she had been no more than a willing female in his bed and she had known that, hadn't she? But it was the cruellest of jokes that his child should have been mixed up with hers.

'Very,' he agreed, his mouth grim, his profile as sculpted as the bronze he was surveying. 'For what it's worth, Annie…' he was turning back to her, his face scored with an emotion she couldn't begin to fathom '…it never was my intention to take you to bed that night,' he told her, as though reading her bruised and battered thoughts, 'or for things to develop the way they did. I don't usually make a habit of sleeping with a woman who's hankering after another man—and especially not one who's already pregnant with that man's child. I should have put a stop to it and I didn't. It was my fault entirely.'

Visibly Annie flinched, feeling as though he had struck her in the solar plexus. He made her feel cheap and more shameless than she already did.

'Please, don't—' Denigrate yourself, she was going to say bitterly, but was stalled by someone coming along the path.

The adoring Elise with an urgent fax message for him, she realised, wondering if the girl had volunteered to bring it out to him. Without a further glance at either of them, Annie pushed past them both and made a hasty retreat to the house.

CHAPTER FOUR

EXPERIMENTING with some new pastels at the table in the elegant drawing room, Annie laid the stick of vivid green colour down on her pad to watch the toddlers at play.

Jack was sitting in the middle of the luxurious carpet, chattering to himself as he concentrated on putting together a wooden jigsaw puzzle. Sean was banging on the base of the empty biscuit tin that had contained the puzzle, keeping up an endless accompaniment of little shouts.

'Yes, all right. I think I get the message.' Annie smiled.

Earlier, Elise had suggested rather curtly that, as it was raining, the boys should play in the nursery, since Felicity Cadman wasn't keen on seeing toys anywhere else in the house. But Brant's mother was out, and so was Brant, Annie thought with a swift rush of insurgence. Besides, she'd wanted to paint the geraniums she could see on the patio, but she wanted to have the children with her as well.

Having grabbed her attention, Sean rushed over to the tall French windows, his chubby fingers splayed on one gleaming pane.

He was louder and more boisterous than Jack, she had observed over the past couple of days since she had been there, and she could see in him much more of Brant than of Naomi. A born leader, she decided. A real little action man, while Jack already showed signs of preferring to quietly think things through.

'Bouncer!' Sean announced suddenly.

She got up from the table, following his little pointing finger to the bundle of grey fur foraging around on the immaculate lawn.

'No, that's not Bouncer, Sean,' Annie told him and glanced down, feeling another tiny hand clutching her trousered leg.

'Quirrel!' Jack stated, having run over to investigate. Looking up at her, he treated Annie to one of his wide, toothy grins.

'Yes, that's right, Jack,' Annie praised softly, bending down to gently ruffle his little mop of dark hair. 'A squirrel,' she repeated, and felt her heart swell with love for him. He was so utterly endearing and he was hers. They were both hers, she thought with an ache of such desperate longing she had to close her eyes against it, take a few deep breaths. Hang on in there, she told herself steadily. Take it as it comes...

The thud of tiny feet opened her eyes. Sean was stooping to grasp one of the chunky wooden shapes that Jack had been playing with. Standing up again, he threw it at Jack. Jack shrieked, and lifted his arms to be picked up.

'Sean!' Annie scolded, responding to Jack's need for immediate comfort. 'That wasn't very nice,' she told him, whereupon he started shrieking too.

With Jack crying in her arms and a still screaming Sean tugging at her skirt, Annie cupped his soft face with her free hand, comforting him too, just as Brant walked in.

'What are they doing? Vying for your attention?' He was sporting that executive image, and amusement lit his eyes as they took in the maternal scene. 'I can't say I blame them,' he remarked with an appreciative glance over her girlish figure beneath the crumpled blouse and jeans that made her heart give a foolish little leap.

'Come here,' he said, striding over to the shrieking Sean, and caught the protesting child determinedly in his arms. After a few moments, though, Sean quietened down. Which was miraculous, because Annie usually had a job placating him once he started. But perhaps he realised he had met his match in Brant, she ruminated enviously—sensed the authority behind the man's gentleness, that will of steel.

'No Bouncer.' Sean was pointing to the window, while Jack struggled in her arms. He wanted his father too. 'No Bouncer.' His lower lip was thrust out as if he was going to cry.

'No, Sean. Bouncer would have him for breakfast.' Brant winked across at Annie. 'What the devil possessed you to saddle the poor creature with a name like that?'

She was rocking Jack now, his wet face buried in her shoulder.

'He was a stray and from the moment he arrived he was determined to keep any other animal from coming into the garden—including next door's Rottweiler.'

A smile tugged at Brant's mouth. 'Quite an intrepid character. And where is he now? Not in tow, I noticed.'

'No.' Annie considered the expensive furnishings just in the room in which they were standing, the luxurious wall-coverings that Naomi had probably chosen, the carpet, the silver brocade suite. His claws would have made short shrift of that sofa! she thought, cringing, but said only, 'He's with Katrina. I thought you...I mean, I didn't think bringing him here would be...well...appropriate.'

'Oh?' His gaze was too probing, and as she glanced away, unsettled, her eyes came to rest with sudden horror low down on the wall behind him. One of the boys must have got hold of her brightest orange pastel stick when she wasn't looking and scribbled on the pearly silk paper! Her paint stick was lying on the floor.

Mortified, quickly she averted her eyes. Whatever was she going to say? 'I'm sorry about the boys being in here. Elise warned me that they weren't supposed to be.' She couldn't stop looking at the incriminating evidence of her carelessness. 'I suppose I should have listened,' she gabbled on, 'but the light was just right in here.' She tore her eyes

back to him. Perhaps he wouldn't notice. 'I just thought...'
She broke off, swallowing.

Half-turned, he had followed her gaze to the obtrusive
scrawl that stood out on its pale background like a flaming
beacon.

'I'm sorry about the wall,' she murmured, biting her
lower lip.

A deep cleft scored his forehead above the hawk-like
nose, making him appear fiercer than ever as he turned back
to her.

'Was it terribly expensive?' she ventured, swallowing to
try and ease the dryness in her throat.

Brant's expression didn't change. 'Terribly.' His lashes
veiled his eyes against whatever it was he was feeling,
thinking. Of perhaps how Naomi had chosen it? Hadn't
Felicity told her that her daughter-in-law had had a free hand
in most of the décor?

'I'm sorry,' she said contritely again. 'I feel dreadful. I
know I shouldn't have let them come in here.'

'And what did you imagine I'd do to you if you did,
Annie? Beat you?'

She stuck her small chin in the air, battling against the
strong desire to defend her actions as well as a creeping,
more insidious tension she wanted to deny as her eyes
clashed with the hard glitter of his.

Suddenly, though, a lazy smile was playing around his
mouth. 'It's only some members of my staff—and perhaps
to a lesser degree my mother,' he said, 'who think children
should only be allowed to run riot in the nursery. I don't
give a toss where they play. In the middle of old Jones's
prize flower bed if they want to.' Old Jones, Annie gathered,
being the stooped and elderly man she had seen tending the
flawless grounds.

'Then you don't mind?' She couldn't believe she was
getting off so lightly.

'The only thing I mind is you treating me as if I was some sort of ogre.' His head jerked up as Sean grabbed at his dark-shadowed jaw. He smiled distractedly at the infant, proving he was anything but. 'I know we lead different lives—perhaps move in different spheres—but it won't convey the perfect atmosphere for our boys if they sense their mother's afraid of their father, will it?'

'Not quite,' Annie uttered meaningfully, disconcerted by the way he had referred to their relationship. But how could anyone describe the situation in any other way? They were each holding their own infant—the infant the other had raised. How could it do anything but bind them in some way? Yet it was a bond with him that for her was too sensually charged, that she didn't welcome or want. 'I'm not afraid of you,' she threw in defiantly then.

'In that case I take it you won't object to coming out with me tonight. One of my recent developments has been enjoying its first year in business and they're having a celebration party tonight. I have a board meeting first, but there's a wonderful gymnasium, pool and solarium that guests can make use of before the party. I'd like you to come with me if you would.'

Annie opened her mouth to refuse, couldn't find the right words and found herself a victim of her own procrastination when he smiled, and said, 'Right, that's settled, then. Nothing too formal. And don't forget your swimwear. We'll be leaving around five forty-five.'

She should have protested, Annie thought later as the warmth of the Jacuzzi foamed and bubbled around her. She should have stood up to him, not let him think he could pull the rug from under her all the time. But the truth was she hadn't been able to resist his offer. It wasn't often she got the chance to visit a Cadman Hotel & Leisure Complex, pamper herself in a spa, dress up, meet new people, enjoy other adult company. More than anything, though, she realised, shamed by her own weakness, it was Brant's company she craved.

But why had he asked her? she wondered, closing her eyes and letting the scented bubbles relax her. He had already told her, that day at the flat, that he didn't want any complications. So perhaps he had simply been at a loose end, with none of his girlfriends—of which he must have quite a few, she deduced grudgingly—able to make it tonight. Or did he, since she was staying under his roof, just feel obliged to ask her?

The thought didn't do much for her ego, any more than her acknowledgement that he had been right earlier. She was afraid of him, or rather of this devastating attraction he still held for her, she decided, which suddenly made her view the evening ahead with trepidation, only as an ordeal she would have to endure.

She felt better after her long, relaxing soak. Refreshed, perfumed and dressed, she met Brant, as previously arranged, in the hotel foyer, which bore the trademark of the Cadman name for its modern luxury.

'You look,' he said hesitantly when he saw her, 'absolutely stunning.'

His compliment sent a surge of warmth singing through her blood.

Why did just a simple compliment from him start her heart pumping? she thought, despairing of herself, but she was glad she had taken time over her appearance.

She was wearing a flowing white top with equally flowing white trousers, her hair twisted up in a way that, while passing for elegance, was redeemed from being too dressy by the loose strands framing her face. She had, however, gone to town with the make-up.

The works! she had decided earlier, her skill with colour creating a blend of purply-red for her lips and nails, and a mauve shading above lashes touched by lengthening mascara, a deeply dramatic look which, with her dark hair and eyes, she always managed to carry off successfully.

Brant's own appearance did nothing to still her racing pulse, because the elegant confines of his immaculate white shirt and dark suit only increased her awareness of the steel-hard masculinity beneath.

'Come on. I want you to meet some of my associates,' he said, offering her his arm, and as soon as they entered the large chandeliered room, Annie knew what it was like to be the centre of attention.

All eyes turned their way, riveted on the physical presence of the man at her side. And it wasn't just female interest that that powerful magnetism claimed. Men, too, especially those who thought his influence might benefit them, tried to emulate him, as Warren had tried, she remembered, feeling the glare of an invisible spotlight, simply because of the man she was with.

'Relax,' he whispered, as though he could sense the tension from the arm tucked inside his. 'There's no reason to feel uncomfortable.'

Wasn't there?

'Just imagine them all naked and wearing red noses.'

It worked. A little laugh, which she had to struggle to contain, bubbled up inside her.

'That's better,' he approved, feeling her relax, and she guessed he would know every trick in the book on how to loosen someone up. And not just someone. A woman, she thought. He would know just what to do. What to say to get her to relax. Respond...

The evening turned out to be less daunting than she had anticipated. His colleagues and business associates were very pleasant and interesting people, accepting Annie without any apparent speculation as to who she might be.

There was a splendid buffet, which she tucked into while

listening to an amusing tale of a lost golf ball from one of Brant's more elderly colleagues, followed by his wife's hilarious story of a canoe holiday they had taken, all which helped pass the time until, for a few short moments, Annie found herself standing alone.

'Well, well. If it isn't my little lost Annie. We probably spend all our time in the city without ever bumping into each other and wind up meeting here, out in glorious suburbia!'

Annie's spirits plummeted as she turned to meet the so obviously handsome face with those hazel eyes that were tugging too familiarly over her.

'I'm not your Annie, Warren,' she said mechanically. 'Not any more.'

'But still just as beautiful.' A rather slick smile told her that he was letting the snub wash over him. In fact, 'slick' seemed to apply to everything about him, Annie found herself noticing now, from his well-groomed tawny hair to that tailored dark suit he'd no doubt selected to show off the results of the long hours he probably still spent working out at the gym. 'So who's the lucky guy these days? Not Cadman, surely?'

Annie followed his gaze to Brant, who was deep in conversation with two attractive women, both probably in their thirties, who had been claiming his attention for the past twenty minutes.

'We're here on business.' After all, that was all this was, wasn't it? she thought. An evening—where Brant was concerned—where it was better to appear with a partner than without.

'And what sort of business would that be exactly?' Warren's voice was suddenly sickly-sweet. 'His PA perhaps? Or are you assisting him in a rather more personal capacity than that? Like keeping his bed warm?'

'Don't be ridiculous!' Annie shot back, her cheeks flaming.

'I was only surmising. It's some special kind of employee who arrives on her boss's arm.' And when she shot him a puzzled look: 'Someone mentioned it,' he informed her, because he hadn't been there when they had arrived, as far as she was aware.

But he was right, of course. If anyone else had thought the same thing, however, then Brant had certainly done nothing since to increase speculation. They had both been chatting—and enjoyably for the most part—with other people for a good deal of the evening, and since Annie knew that for Brant this wasn't just a social affair, she hadn't minded at all, until now.

'So how's life treating you, Warren?' she asked, ignoring his last statement. 'And where's the lovely Caroline? That was her name, wasn't it?' As if she could forget! She sent a searching glance over his shoulder, pretending to look for the striking blonde for whom she had been jilted.

He shrugged. 'We're just friends nowadays.'

'You mean it didn't work out.'

He hesitated before answering. 'She wanted to get married. I didn't.'

'That's a familiar scenario!' If she sounded bitter, she couldn't help it.

'I'm sorry,' he said.

'Sorry?' She gave a brittle little laugh. 'For what, pray?'

'I wasn't ready. I got scared. Cold feet, I think they call it.'

'Really? I think the more appropriate term would be a frozen heart!'

'All right, I deserved that. I was wrong. I admit it. But I'd like to make it up to you, if you'd let me.'

The hum of conversation and laughter in the large room was blurred by the anger and amazement which blanketed all else, except the rather cloying spice of Warren's after-shave lotion.

'I wouldn't dream of putting you to the trouble!' she snapped, and saw his mouth suddenly tighten.

'I said I was sorry.'

'That's right, you did. And what am I supposed to do? Fall down on my knees and show my undying gratitude for it? Well, I'm sorry, too, Warren.' She even managed a smile. 'But you're going to have to find some other sad creature to waste her time and affections on you, because it isn't going to be me!'

Involuntarily, she glanced towards Brant, the remnants of her forced smile still evident. She caught his hard, contemplative regard, saw something flare for a second in the green-gold of his eyes. But then one of the women said something to him and he turned away, leaving Annie feeling oddly—stupidly—bereft.

'What are you hoping for, Annie? To try and catch him between marriages? Doesn't seem to be working, does it?' Warren sneered, clearly smarting from being given the brush-off.

But then he had noticed her with Brant at that last party, she thought, cringing; noticed her, as she had intended him to when she had flirted so outrageously and shamefully with their mutual employer solely to try and hide her broken heart.

'I really don't know what you're talking about,' Annie bluffed, stealing another unconscious glance at Brant from beneath her lashes. He was totally engrossed in whatever the taller and more striking of the two women was saying and Annie was startled to recognise a cruel, sharp jab of jealousy.

'What is it you find so attractive? That rather ruthless look about him?' Warren had caught her reluctant interest in the other man and from his satisfied smile was well aware how she was feeling. 'His power? They say it's a hell of an aphrodisiac. Or is it the thought of all that lovely money?'

As much as she was annoyed by Warren's remarks, his pursuit of the subject was disconcerting her beyond belief, and hotly she retorted, 'Not everyone shares your own lack of scruples, Warren!'

'Then start to grow up and realise it for yourself.' He slipped a hand into the pocket of his pristine suit, looking down on her as though she were a child. 'You're just a fill-in, Annie. That guy's way out of your league. I would have thought you'd be setting your sights on something more certain in your situation.'

A passing waiter, seeing the empty glass she'd forgotten she was holding, offered her a refill. She shook her head, and watched Warren take one from the tray.

'What do you mean?' She looked at him obliquely. 'My situation?'

Warren sipped, swallowed, savoured, produced that slick, smooth smile. 'Someone told me you had a kid.'

Annie felt herself stiffen with tension, and through it the tug of something sharply maternal. She needed to be with Sean—with Sean and Jack. She had already been away too long.

'Yes,' she said cagily, holding her breath as she saw one tawny eyebrow arch.

'What did you do? Meet some dashing Mediterranean lover while you were abroad…what was it? Pea-picking?'

Clearly he wanted to make things seem as derogatory as possible, and for a moment the pain of a well-remembered anguish clawed at her heart. He had treated her badly, but she had survived it; could only be grateful now that he had jilted her. Seeing him here only made her wonder at her shaming lack of judgement, wonder what she had ever seen in him, how she could have been so naïve not to have seen through the gloss to the raw primer of insincerity beneath.

But, mercifully, it seemed she could be spared the worst kind of humiliation, that of his asking any more awkward questions, because evidently he had no clear idea of when her baby had been born. Wouldn't even suspect...

'You'd probably be best advised to entertain your neglected customers, Maddox.' A deep voice at her shoulder made Annie turn quickly. 'Otherwise we could all find ourselves picking up peas instead of pay-cheques at the end of the year.'

Had he heard the things Warren had been saying? she wondered, mortified, noticing how suddenly diminished and deflated her ex-fiancé looked both in stature and in mood by Brant's formidable authority. Was he feeling sorry for her? Was that what had made him say that? Or was that rough edge she had detected in his voice generated by something else?

'You're right, sir.' Annie's skin crawled from the sycophantic smile Warren flashed at the man who paid his wages, the mock-sincerity that three years ago might have fooled her as he said, 'It's nice to see you again, Annie. We'll have to meet up. Perhaps for lunch some time.'

She watched his swift retreat with guarded eyes, half-afraid to look at Brant, whose dark mood she could feel enveloping her like an angry storm.

'Get your things,' he rasped, pulling the glass she still held out of her grasp and dumping it down on the nearest table. 'We're leaving.'

Determined fingers at her elbow were already ushering her towards the cloakroom, where she had left her wet swimwear and the clothes she had arrived in. And she thought, What has he got to sound so angry about? It's me who's had to suffer all the embarrassment and humiliation. Not him!

'You knew he'd be there, didn't you?' she accused when they were travelling in silence back to his huge, intimidating house. Hopelessly she longed for the safe informality of her little flat. 'You just wanted me to come with you tonight because you knew he'd be there. Why Brant? To get some sort of kick out of seeing how I'd react?'

'Don't be ridiculous,' he said, the lights from oncoming traffic on the other side of the carriageway chasing shadows across his face. 'I didn't think you'd be in danger of bumping into Sean's—I mean Ja—' He uttered a small invective under his breath. 'Your child's father.' From that swift amendment it was clear he still had difficulty accepting that the infant he had been bringing up for the past two years wasn't his own. 'Do you think I want to complicate things more than they already are? OK, Maddox still works for me, but I didn't imagine for one moment that he would be there. He probably got a free ride on someone else's back! Anyway, what's so terrible about meeting him, Annie?' He had slowed down to take a left turning, his headlights illuminating a sign for villages through which they had passed on their way to the complex. 'Unless, of course, you've been lying to me and to yourself all along and you're still carrying a torch for him.'

Strands of dark hair caressed Annie's face as she looked at him, aghast. 'Do you really think I'm that stupid? Credit me with some sense, please!' She was affronted by anyone suggesting she might still want someone as deceitful and insincere as Warren was. 'I detest the man!'

Brant switched off the wiper blades because the rain that had persisted all day and turned to drizzle by the time they had left the hotel had finally stopped. They were moving through a rural lane overhung with trees, headlights cutting through the darkness, gleaming on the wet road.

'Said with real conviction.' The deep tones were overlaid with sarcasm. 'Is that why you looked so pleased to have him chatting you up?'

Was that what he thought?

'I couldn't have been happier!' she snapped, matching his sarcasm syllable for syllable. 'And anyway, what did you care? You were so tied up with your own adoring admirer, you scarcely spoke two words to me all night!'

'So that's it,' he said silkily and, too late, she realised the folly of her words because he was pulling over into a small break in the hedgerow, bringing the car to a standstill beside a large five-bar gate. He turned off the vehicle's lights, plunging them into the intimate, engulfing darkness. 'If it's my attention you want, you only had to say.'

CHAPTER FIVE

A WARNING flashed in Annie's dark eyes. Her heart seemed to be thumping out of control.

'No, Brant!' she protested, in an attempt to stave off the inevitable. 'This isn't a good idea.'

She heard the soft leather seat squeak beneath his weight.

'Oh, yes, Annie,' he breathed, leaning over, reaching for her, 'I rather think it is.'

He had kissed her before—at the flat. Even made love to her on that fated night that could have been yesterday or a million years ago. But nothing could prepare her for the sensations that assailed her this time as his mouth descended over hers.

His kiss was like a homecoming, a stark recognition and acceptance of where she belonged. The feel and taste and scent of him and those strong hands sliding over her body were stamped on her consciousness as indelibly as her own signature and she yielded to them, uttering a small, soft sigh of acquiescence.

She could feel the tension in him beneath the dark jacket as her arms slid around him. His jaw was slightly rough against hers, even though he had probably shaved only a few hours before, and the subtle scent of his lotion, mingling with the more personal musk of his skin, was acting on Annie like a potent drug.

They were both breathing hard and erratically when he lifted his head.

'You seduced me under Maddox's nose before. Responded to me as wildly as any woman could respond to

71

a man. And you still respond to me,' he whispered. 'So beautifully.'

He kissed the side of her mouth, her chin, his lips feather-light across her skin before he dipped his head to taste the perfumed softness of her throat.

She was locked in a private world with him, murmuring small sounds of pleasure into the silence. In the intimate warmth her ears registered the occasional creak of the car's engine cooling down, the burr of distant traffic on the main carriageway.

Her eyes growing accustomed to the darkness, she caught her breath from the sheer masculinity of him leaning across her, from the exciting strength of his hard frame, and all that he had the power to do to her, because he was right.

She had gone to bed with him before, thinking herself in love with Warren Maddox, but just one night in Brant's arms and any feeling for the other man had faded like the moon on a summer morning.

'In whatever way you want him, it's still me you want to be kissing you, isn't it?' he said hoarsely, reading her darkest secrets. 'Still me you want to fire those wild passions of yours. Still me who you want to take you to bed.'

'No,' she breathed in protest, which was ludicrous, she realised, even as she uttered it. But she was terrified and shamed by the strength of her own attraction to him, by the fact that any man could make her such a hapless victim of her own desire.

'No?' She could hear the smile in his voice, then with mind-blowing deliberation he lowered his head and showed her just how wrong she was when he parted the deep V of her virginal white top for his tongue to lick a fiery path along the scented valley between her breasts, bringing her straining towards him with a small groan of need.

Beneath the flimsy top her breasts ached for his rough, skilled hands, craving their calloused warmth against their tender peaks, while sharp needles of wanting pierced her lower body.

'No?' he taunted again, raising his head to look at her as she flopped back against the headrest. Her hair had come loose about her shoulders and her eyes were dark and slumberous beneath the long strands of her fringe. 'Who are you kidding, Annie? Unless,' he challenged, with a sudden rough edge to his voice, 'you're so desperate for Maddox that any man will do to ease your frustration.'

'You really believe that?' she objected, her voice husky from the frustration he had spoken of—that he alone had brought about—but also because he could even suggest what he had.

He didn't answer, but this time when he took her in his arms and kissed her it was with almost punishing possession.

'Perhaps it's time you forgot him, Annie,' he rasped when he allowed her up for air, finally released her. 'Maybe what you need is a lesson in some good, hard loving to drive that social-climbing opportunist out of your mind.'

And who'll drive you out of my mind when you've finished with me? she wondered bitterly, feeling an acute throb of desire stab her loins just from imagining herself pinned naked beneath him in some bed.

'And those adoring admirers, as you called them,' he said softly, sitting back in his seat and turning the key in the ignition, 'are the partners of two of my biggest customers—nothing more.'

Which told her, she thought, feeling reprimanded, yet ridiculously relieved too as he pulled out onto the road. And that was utterly, utterly stupid, she told herself vehemently. There was too much at stake to risk inviting any sort of an affair with him. It would only complicate things, as he had so rightly said that day in her flat. Apart from which, she had vowed never to allow herself to be hurt by any man ever again.

She had recovered from Warren's betrayal a long time ago, but an involvement with Brant—well, that would be a totally different matter.

One night with him—that was all she had had. But every instinct of self-preservation warned her that if she did get emotionally involved with him it would take far longer, if ever, to bounce back again when he abandoned her—as he most probably would, as the others had. Because she had to admit to herself now that although what they had shared had just been one casual, if glorious, night, she had never quite managed to get Brant Cadman out of her system.

There were raised voices in the hall. As the spin cycle of the washing machine in the large utility room whirred to a halt, Annie could clearly hear what was being said.

'…And I don't keep a whole collection in the wardrobe, Mother, like Beau blasted Brummell! You know I hate the things.'

A moment's silence seemed to indicate a long-suffering sigh from Felicity.

'Yes, dear. But don't swear in front of the servants. It isn't nice.'

'It's enough to make a man swear if he comes home to find his laundry constantly being lost!'

'Not constantly, Brant.' Felicity's tones were softly conciliatory. 'It's only happened once before with one of your other dress shirts. And the girl has apologised.'

Starting to empty her small spun load into a laundry basket, Annie caught the sound of a third voice, young, muffled, apologetic.

Brant was in a mood, she thought with a little shudder, feeling sorry for whoever was on the receiving end of his temper. She couldn't blame him though, for getting annoyed, if his staff were inefficient enough to keep losing his shirts.

A second later and a flushed young maid rushed into the room and out through the door up to the servants' quarters. It was evident that she was crying, Annie realised, hearing her scurrying up the rear stairs.

She had sneaked in here earlier, wanting to launder a few of Sean's things. She hated troubling the servants and had chosen a quiet period during the afternoon when no one else was around.

She was still bending to her task when she noticed the superbly-clad long legs of the man dominating the doorway.

'Where did she go?' Brant demanded, and so brusquely that Annie felt her hackles rise.

Straightening, she shook her tousled hair out of her eyes.

'She? Who's she?' she enquired rather too snappily, because his arrogance and the sheer impact of him standing there in a light-grey suit, white shirt and silver tie wasn't doing a lot for her composure.

He gave her a 'Don't take that tone with me' sort of look, took a breath as though to gather himself and then said, still rather impatiently, 'The young girl who just ran through here. You must have seen her.'

'Oh! The one you were bullying, you mean.'

A dark eyebrow shot up, and Annie tensed. Whatever was she thinking of? she chided herself.

'Bullying?' He took a few measured strides towards her. 'Is that what it sounded like?'

Stooping to pick up several items from the basket, Annie didn't answer, starting to fold them neatly on top of the washing machine. Sean's little red checked shirt. Her purple sun-top. A little pair of navy-blue dungarees.

'I'm not accusing you of anything.' She was shaking out several pairs of little multicoloured socks, starting to feel decidedly unkempt in her stretchy cream top and jeans against his impeccable style. 'Unlike you with your staff.'

'All right. Perhaps I was rather rough on her,' he acceded rather surprisingly, 'but it's exasperating enough having to attend a charity function in formal gear without the only infernal shirt I'd consider wearing going mysteriously astray. It's already…' impatiently he consulted his watch, exposing a good deal of strong, tanned wrist. Tanned from the holiday he had taken with Jack, which turn of events had started all this, resulted in him coming to find her. To claim his son. Her son '…ten past six. Excuse me for not observing the niceties, but we have to be there at seven sharp.'

We? Annie knew Felicity had one of her poetry-reading meetings that evening, and Brant hadn't invited *her* to go anywhere with him tonight. So perhaps he had a date, arranged before he had invited her here, Annie thought. But there again, perhaps it was since.

'How do you know it was with your laundry anyway? Perhaps it's still hanging in your wardrobe,' she suggested tartly, and then, unable to help herself, driven by a red-hot emotion, 'or perhaps you left it somewhere else altogether!'

She reached down and grabbed a couple more items, dumping them on top of the machine. A little pair of corded burgundy trousers, which she folded unceremoniously down on top of the socks, before snatching up a pink cotton blouse.

Pink cotton blouse?

She held up the item to inspect it, saw the expensive designer label below the very masculine collar and felt her heart sink in dismay.

'You were saying, Annie?' Soft mockery infiltrated the voice, so close he had to be standing right behind her.

She swung round, and found that he was. She looked

down at the ruined garment, then back at Brant again, her eyes disbelieving, her mouth a round 'o' of surprise.

'I didn't...I mean...I don't know...' Oh, gosh! Whatever could she say to him? She had accused him of wrongly chastising his servants and negligence, even implied he'd been sleeping around! And all the time it had been her... 'It—it must have been in the machine...' she stammered, gesturing lamely towards the appliance.

'Evidently.'

'...When I took the previous load out.'

A deep line drew his thick brows together. 'When you what?'

Oh, God! she thought. Now he'll think I'm meddling in his domestic affairs as well as ruining his expensive shirts.

'There was a wash in there that had already finished.' And which someone had since whisked away to be dried and ironed, she realised, glancing hopelessly round the room with all its time-saving equipment. 'I had to take everything out.'

'Obviously not everything.'

Annie bit her lip. He wasn't looking the least bit pleased.

'It must have been stuck to the drum and I didn't see it.'

'Well, didn't you spin it round to check...' he cast a disparaging look at the little pile of clothes she had just folded '...before you put your kaleidoscopic assortment of Dayglo wear in?'

God, he was angry!

'Of course I did!' she stressed heatedly, but she couldn't honestly swear to it. Not for certain. The fact that he would have, when she might have overlooked to do so, needled, yet surprised her as well—until she remembered that some time during the past week he had told her how he had looked after himself during and for a few years after leaving university. Perhaps it wasn't so surprising after all.

Pushing a strand of loose hair behind an ear, unable to

resist it now, she held the sorry-looking shirt against the impeccably tailored suit and said tentatively, 'It could look rather fetching with grey.'

Something tugged at his mouth. Was he amused? She didn't think so.

'Look, I'm sorry,' she uttered, mortified. First the wall. Now this! 'Didn't you ever ruin anything, Mr Perfect? Didn't Naomi?'

For a moment, when she saw his jaw tighten, she wondered if she had gone too far. But then he said smoothly, 'As far as I know, Naomi left everything to the servants.' *As you should.* He didn't say it, but she guessed that was what he was thinking.

'Well, perhaps I'm not so adept as you are—' or Naomi was, she appended silently '—at pushing other people around!' When she caught the look he shot her, she said, 'OK, then. Telling them what to do!'

'It's their job—looking after the house—for which I pay them very well,' he told her. 'And I'm quite sure my staff don't look upon themselves as being pushed around.' He removed the shirt unceremoniously from her grasp.

'I'm sorry,' she reiterated, frustrated because not only had she ruined his best dress-shirt, but she also had no way of making recompense. She could tell from its label the sort of sum it would have cost. There was no way she could hope to replace it out of the money she made from her paintings, so she didn't even bother to suggest it. 'I'll go and apologise to that poor girl,' she offered instead, 'for getting her into trouble.'

'I'll speak to her,' he stated decisively. 'After all, as you so eloquently pointed out, it was I who upset her.'

So he wasn't above apologising to a junior member of his staff, even though it was all her fault that the problem had arisen.

And that's that, she thought unhappily, watching with

guarded eyes as he turned away from her and, on his way out, flipped the lid of a plastic waste receptacle that was standing near the door, dropping the ruined garment inside.

'Hang the shirt,' he muttered, almost under his breath, and to her surprise was crossing the room towards her again. 'What's really troubling you, Annie?'

Did she seem troubled?

Her throat worked nervously and, unsettled by him, she stooped to pick up the last remaining item in the laundry basket to give her hands something to do. Unfortunately it was one of her G-strings, her black silk one, and quickly she dropped it onto the folded pile as if it were a hot coal.

Brant's mouth quirked, his dark lashes lowered as he regarded the tantalising little garment. 'Aren't you happy with our arrangement?'

She wished she could say she was. Even so, she couldn't begin to tell him why she wasn't.

'Is there anything you need? Want? Anything or… anyone…you miss?'

What was he thinking? she wondered, feeling those clear, probing eyes studying her every response. That she was hankering after some boyfriend? Warren Maddox perhaps?

'I just want everything to be as certain as it used to be,' she began, and once she had started found she couldn't stop. 'I want to be able to get up in the mornings and find I'm able to work—because I can't! I just can't focus—and haven't been able to since I realised my baby was not mine but some other woman's! I want to feel I can move without breaking some golden rule in your perfect palace of a house! And yes, since you mention it, there is someone I miss. I miss him very much. My cat!'

During her little outburst, myriad emotions had chased across his face ranging from sympathetic concern to anger and now… What was it? Annie wondered. Relief? But why? What was he worried about? That she might suddenly take off with some boyfriend who might be lurking in the wings and take Sean with her? Or was he worried she might run off with Jack as well?

'So many wants,' he mocked softly, 'and instead you find yourself living with an insufferable bully who beats his servants and rules you with an iron hand, is that it?'

Amusement was crinkling the corners of his eyes, making him appear younger, more approachable. But she could feel his closeness as a tangible warmth, that very personal scent of him making her head spin, do funny things to her stomach, and so rather shakily she said, 'I didn't accuse you of anything so drastic—apart from the bullying bit. I just think in future you could pick on someone your own size—who'd be a much better match for you.'

'Like you, you mean?' He slipped his hand under her hair, causing a sensual little shiver to run through her. She felt the touch of those long fingers against her neck, the palm that cupped her jaw, smooth and warm and dangerously erotic. 'Annie in fiery mode. Annie with all guns blazing.'

'I was talking physically.' Darn! Why did she have to sound like a croaking frog?

'So am I. And you know as well as I do...' he stooped and kissed the corner of her mouth, making her breath lock in her lungs '...you're just my size, Annie. Small you might be, but from past experience I seem to remember we fit together very well.' His lips were so gentle, his breath so sensual against her cheek, she had a job reminding herself that he had said he was going out—possibly with another woman. That she was nothing more, would be nothing more, to him than she had ever been, if she was to allow it—just a pleasurable distraction in his life.

She tried to move back, felt the cold, hard bulk of the washing machine, like a conspirator, effectively trapping her there for him. But his voice was so soft, the sight and scent of him so deadly seductive that when he ran his tongue along her jaw-line to the sensitive aperture of her ear she sucked in a sharp breath and felt her body respond in reckless, traitorous arousal.

'Like peas in a pod,' that deep voice continued to torment, and dazedly she wondered if he had chosen that simile as a reminder to her of his effective supremacy over Warren. 'Like a hand in a glove. Not an iron hand but a velvet one that wants to caress you until you're begging me to release you from the tortuous ecstasy of it just as you did before. But unfortunately I have to go out...' he drew a harsh, ragged breath '...and you aren't making it very easy for me.'

He straightened, though his fingers still played lightly across her throat.

Annie lowered her lashes against the eroticism of his touch, against the disappointment burning in her eyes as she blurted out, 'That's right. You mustn't keep her waiting, must you?'

Brant's chest expanded beneath the sleek grey jacket.

'Jealousy?' he taunted silkily. 'I really must do something to curb that unnecessary little streak. Do you really think I could touch you like this, say these things to you, if I had another woman waiting for me?'

Yes! Because you did it before! all her senses screamed bitterly, but she didn't say it.

His hand fell away from her, and with his face turning serious now he said, 'It's a charity fund-raising dinner, Annie, at which I'm the principal speaker. And it's definitely all male, I'm afraid. So unless you want to risk doing to a lot of potent, red-blooded businessmen what you have no difficulty doing to me, I suggest you curl up with a good book and stay here under my roof, where it's safe, and where I can at least leave you alone without wondering where that blazing sexuality of yours is going to land you.

Take you with me, and I can promise you, you'd be eaten alive.'

Reluctantly affected by his awareness of her, watching him stride away, she wanted to kick herself for feeling so pleased he wasn't meeting another woman.

'And Annie,' unexpectedly, he turned in the doorway, bringing guilty colour rushing into her cheeks, 'next time you go to Katrina's, for heaven's sake, bring back that cat.'

She fetched Bouncer from her friend's home the very next day and brought him back to the magnificent house, mewing loudly from his wicker basket at the indignity of it all.

Sean and Jack were thrilled. Especially Jack, Annie was touched to see, who had never had a pet of his own. No sooner was it out of its basket, however, than the tabby, frightened by the onslaught of two sets of eager little hands, raced out of the nursery and down the stairs to the kitchen, where it took up immediate residence on top of the split-level cooker housing and refused to budge.

'Doesn't look too happy with things, does he?' Brant, who had been in the hall when Annie had come in and watched the whole proceedings, now observed drily. 'A bit like his mother.' And with a sideways, disconcerting glance at her, he added silkily, 'I'm sure in the long run, all it will take will be a bit of gentle handling.'

He was walking away before she had a chance to open her mouth.

The next week or so passed relatively smoothly. The hospital had begun an investigation into how the two boys could have been switched at birth and were also recommending that DNA tests be carried out to ensure that the babies had been substituted only for each other and that there were no other parties involved.

'That's crazy!' Annie exclaimed when Brant told her. She

was still confused, bewildered, angry over what had been allowed to happen in the first place. 'How could they have been mixed up with anybody else's baby?' Someone she had never heard of. Someone else neither of them knew. It was a nightmare enough discovering that the child you'd brought up belonged to someone who at least wasn't a perfect stranger, someone you knew, could respect and accept. Now this... She didn't want the test done, and she told him so.

'I understand how you feel, Annie, but it's so obvious Jack's yours. I told you before—any further tests would only be a formality in his case. But Sean...' They were strolling in the garden, alone, as both toddlers were in bed. The late-evening sun, setting fire to the tall trees behind the lawns, vividly accentuated the contained emotion that scored Brant's face. 'I could kid myself forever that he looks like me. That he got his hair and colouring from his mother. But how will I know for sure? I've been told that my son—that Jack—isn't mine. If I'm to accept that, then I have to know for certain that the child you were given by mistake is. Mine and Naomi's. That he's really the child she died giving birth to. I owe it to her, for God's sake!'

Something inexplicably acute twisted inside Annie.

They had reached the point by the hedge where the bronze sculpture stood serenely on her plinth. Touched by the evening sun, her smooth, polished surface and perfect features seemed to Annie to come alive. She glanced towards Brant. He must have been thinking the same thing, she thought, because his strong, rugged face was marked by some private inner struggle, shutting her out of a world she had no place in and no right to enter. She felt excluded, oddly desolate. But the fact that Sean might not be his either had never occurred to her, and a double dose of anguish tore through her.

'It's all right for you! You haven't brought him up! You

haven't nursed him when he's been sick and comforted him when he's cried, watched him cut his first tooth. I couldn't bear it if they said he wasn't yours! I'd feel I'd lost him completely!'

She had dragged his attention back to her, reluctantly, she imagined, at first. But now, as though he'd given himself a mental shake, those glittering eyes, sharp as ever, were narrowing into hard, probing slits.

'I mean...I know you,' she uttered quickly, afraid that her little outburst would convey more to him than she was ready to admit to herself.

'No, you don't,' he said, with a no more than casual glance back now towards the bronze. The light had faded from it already, leaving it lifeless and cold. Back in her world, Brant wore the mask of a stoic, like one resigned to his fate. 'All it will take is your permission, Annie,' he murmured, and with such remarkable gentleness that she had no choice but to give in.

The result wasn't instant. Everything, it seemed, was going to take time. Getting used to the situation. The day when she would be able to leave Brant's elegant house and resume her old life—though under what arrangement for the boys, she couldn't imagine. The DNA test. And that was perhaps the worst of all.

'You might think this little Jack looks like you, but it's easy to imagine anything—especially in babies,' her mother pointed out when Annie telephoned her early the following morning. 'I still say Sean's ours. You'll see.' Jane Talbot still refused to believe anything else, which made trying to come to terms with things herself so much harder, Annie thought. After all, her parents hadn't seen little Jack, because the photographs that Brant had provided for her to send to them had still not reached them, and they couldn't know what it was like to be so torn between two infants.

She needed help in adjusting and her mother's refusal even to come to terms with her daughter's predicament wasn't helping matters at all.

Her parents weren't happy either, knowing that she had been so quick to move in with Brant, although it was her mother who openly expressed it.

'I mean...who is he? What do you *know* about him? Your father and I are very concerned about it.'

'Don't be,' Annie returned impatiently, wanting to wind up the conversation. 'I used to work with him. For him. Well, not for him exactly. He was the big boss. The king pin. I never saw him. Well, only once or twice. He's nice.'

Which was the most inaccurate word to describe a man of Brant's forceful and powerful persona, Annie thought after a less taxing conversation with her father. Charismatic. Intelligent. Intimidating. But nothing anywhere as mundane as nice!

With Brant somewhere in the city, Felicity visiting a friend and Elise having taken the children on a picnic, that day Annie attempted some sketches of the garden from her bedroom window, then wound up throwing them all away.

Later, finding herself alone still after helping Elise put the boys to bed, she made another attempt at getting her creative juices flowing. Nothing worked, though, no matter how hard she tried and, with the earlier conversation with her mother still unsettling her, and feeling totally defeated by her lack of productivity, she decided to go downstairs and see how Bouncer was doing.

He had been mewing to go outside ever since he had arrived and she had been cautious about letting him. He had, however, had a week now to get used to his new surroundings, she calculated, recalling someone saying that the best way to make sure a cat returned to a strange house was to butter its paws. Which was going to be easy, she thought, when she found the tabby curled up asleep on a chair in the kitchen.

She was grateful when one of the kitchen staff offered to help, and all would have been fine if someone hadn't dropped a saucepan lid just as she was carrying the cat towards the back door. It was his sudden struggling and her frantic attempts to hang on to him that caused all the damage, when an extended claw caught in a tea-towel that was overhanging one of the work surfaces with a moulded plastic dish sitting on top.

It wasn't her fault that the jelly wasn't set. Or that Bouncer, having pulled the whole thing down on top of him, darted out of the kitchen and through the nearest escape route, which just happened to be the open door to the exquisite drawing room.

Running in after him, she was just in time to see the cat scrambling off the sofa, where, she realised to her horror, he must have stopped to shake himself in indignation.

Now, standing mortified in the middle of the deep Persian rug, Annie stared, open-mouthed, at the blobs of tangerine slime sliding slowly down the back of the settee, and the various orange spots spattered indiscriminately all over its silvery upholstery. Two discarded mandarin slices were clinging to one of the cushions.

It was Felicity Cadman's uncharacteristic little shriek that brought Annie's eyes swivelling towards the doorway.

Brant's mother had already disappeared—Annie could hear her calling urgently down the hallway for one of the servants—but Brant hadn't. He was looming, larger than life, only a few feet away from her. Vaguely now, she recalled his mother asking if he would pick her up on his way home.

His jaw seemed clenched as he surveyed the sorry state of his furniture. The furniture he and Naomi had probably picked out together, Annie thought, swallowing. His eyes, though, were dark and inscrutable as they clashed with hers.

'It was the cat,' she tried to explain, gesturing hopelessly towards the sofa. 'I wanted...I thought...I mean, I tried to let him out...' Already she could hear voices, footsteps echoing back to them along the hall.

'Not soon enough, obviously.' Brant's words were clipped and dry.

Annie shrugged, looking around from beneath the dark strands of her fringe. The blasted animal was nowhere to be seen. 'I'm sorry.'

'As you seem to need to keep saying to me. Constantly.' His mouth compressed as he cast another disparaging glance at the slimy sofa and back at Annie again. 'Do you always cause utter chaos wherever you go?'

Annoyed with herself for what he must think of her, Annie was about to apologise again, then remembered that he had ridiculed her for that already. Shrugging again, she said, far more nonchalantly than she felt, 'You learn to live with it.'

An eyebrow arched in mocking scepticism. 'Somehow I can't imagine it.' He added grimly, 'It is, however, what I'd like to talk to you about.'

So this was it! Eviction, she thought, and knew a sudden surge of panic. What was going to happen about Sean? And Jack?

Felicity had returned with Elise and another girl carrying bowls and sponges and what looked like cleaning agents, Annie noted, feeling utterly responsible for giving everyone so much work to do. From the rather snooty way Elise looked at her, the French girl was thinking along the same lines. Annie was unable to miss the covert glance she stole at Brant, before Felicity started issuing her instructions.

'Well, Mother...' That masculine mouth curved, but the

eyes he turned on Annie glittered with the promise of atonement. 'Do you want to give her a spanking or shall I?'

She darted an indignant look at him. How dared he talk to her like that? And in front of his employees too! She heard the second girl giggle, caught the smug look on Elise's face and the slight flush to her skin that told Annie she'd probably view such treatment from her intensely masculine boss as anything but a punishment. Well, *she* didn't have the same subservient opinion!

'Annie, come with me.'

Before she had realised it, his fingers were at her elbow, steering her swiftly out of the room. She felt like an offending pupil being led away to the headmaster's study for six of the best.

She took a nervous gulp when she realised that that was exactly where he had brought her, her eyes making a swift assessment of a very tidy desktop, the low studded leather couch and heavy curtains, an amalgam of greens and brass and mahogany. Her heart pounded in her breast as she heard him closing the door behind them.

'What shall I do?' she threw at him, tugging out of his grasp. He looked so big and daunting and angry. He had to be angry. 'Bend over the desk?'

'Well...' Strangely he looked amused by that remark. 'It could make for an interesting development.' Despite everything, something feral flared in his eyes, weakening her defences, the power of him with that raw animal magnetism undermining her confidence. And of course she had made a total fool of herself—again!

Framed by a floor-to-ceiling bookcase, he was standing with his arms folded. What did that signify? she wondered, trembling. A firm stand? A totally negative attitude towards her? Well, if he was going to issue her with her notice, she was going to make it easy on him. And on herself!

'This house...it isn't me.'

'I entirely agree.'

He did? 'I'm always doing something wrong.'

'You're darn right, you are.'

Something other than just wounded pride caused her brow to furrow. He didn't have to agree quite so readily, did he?

'We're wrecking the place.'

'That's an understatement.'

'OK. So I'll pay you back.'

'And how, pray, do you propose to do that, Annie? I believe that sofa cost an arm and a leg.'

Annie stiffened. 'Thanks for pointing it out to me!' Of all the mean, insensitive oafs!

'Don't mention it.'

'Oh, I'll mention it,' she countered, hurt, 'every day until I've paid my debt in full! Maybe I can't offer you an arm or a leg. But perhaps you'd like to take your pound of flesh from somewhere else!'

She was being sarcastic, of course, but only realised the folly of her words when his lips curled in a sensual smile and he said, 'Now, there's an offer no man in his right mind could refuse.'

Arms unfolded, he was moving away from the bookcase and something like a warning lit her eyes. He wasn't surely thinking that she...?

'I was hardly serious!' she snapped in an effort to stall him. 'Just because I was misguided enough to jump into bed with you before doesn't mean I'd ever be crazy enough to do it again! You want me out of your beautiful house. Isn't that what you brought me here to tell me? Well, all right, I'll go. I'll get Sean's and my things together and be off the premises within the hour!'

'You'll do no such thing!'

She had started across the carpet, but now he was barring her way and she had to stop short to avoid colliding with the hard wall of his body.

'What?'

'You aren't taking Sean anywhere. Certainly not at this time of the day.'

Her eyes darted after his to the brass clock on the mantelpiece. It was nearly half-past seven. 'He's my son.'

'No, he isn't.'

Fear trickled through her like hot, hardening tar.

'I brought him up. He's mine. And I'll fight you for him in court if I have to!'

'Annie…'

'No court of law would let you keep him!'

'Annie.'

'Not if they knew you'd tricked me into—'

'Annie! *Annie!*'

The hard emphasis silenced her. She was white, trembling with emotion.

'There's a far better solution to battling it out and dragging each other through the courts—our children's names into the papers. So far we've managed to avoid that,' he reminded her. He spoke quietly, cleverly gearing his tone—his manner—to bring her under control, she realised, resenting him for his cool manipulation because it worked—just.

'What do you mean?' she queried, calmer now.

His chest lifted and fell beneath the crisp whiteness of his shirt. 'I think we should get married,' he said.

CHAPTER SIX

'WHAT?' Annie whispered, unsure whether she had heard him properly.

'We should get married,' he repeated as casually as if he had been talking about the weather.

'But we aren't...I mean...' She didn't know what she meant. A proposal from him was the last thing she had been expecting. 'I'm not ready to get married,' she uttered rather lamely, still shocked by his unbelievable suggestion.

'Is anyone ever really...ready?'

Had he been? The first time? she wondered abstractedly, but didn't even need to dwell on it. He'd loved the woman he had married and still did. No, that ridiculing note in his voice was from his frustration with her.

'But we live in totally different worlds. It wouldn't work.'

'Not so different, Annie—and we could make it work.'

Could they? Crazily, she found herself fighting a strong urge to accept.

'But we don't...I mean...you don't...' Love me, she almost said, and wondered why. Did she love him? Surely not! 'I don't love you,' she blurted out, driven by the fear of just how strong her feelings might really be.

A muscle twitched in the hard jaw. 'I'm not asking you to. There are marriages of convenience taking place every day—all over the world—without love. And you must admit that a marriage between the two of us wouldn't be so much a convenience as expedient.'

Expedient. She had looked it up once. One definition her dictionary had given was 'a means of attaining one's end'.

Well, what had she expected? she thought, berating herself for the ache that seemed to concentrate itself around her middle. A declaration of his devotion? The affected, bended-knee touch that she had got from Warren?

'Maybe I'm not promising you what Maddox promised,' he said somewhat hoarsely and with disconcerting shrewdness, 'but then neither do I renege on my promises. It might not be everything you would have wished, but I can promise you you'll be adequately satisfied in other areas.'

Oh, dear heaven! If she thought of going to bed with him, spending night after night in the clutches of raw passion while he drove her mindless with his expert lovemaking, she could easily be swayed. And she mustn't—couldn't accept him on those terms! Because, of course, what he wanted was to stop her walking out of here with Naomi's son, and he was prepared to go to any lengths to prevent it—even if it meant marrying her.

She lifted her chin, a defensive little gesture against everything he was proposing. 'Sex isn't everything.'

'True,' he agreed, that proud head tilting in concurrence, 'but it's a hell of a starting point when all you've got are two little kiddies who desperately need two parents.'

Feeling her defences being gnawed at, resolutely she uttered, 'It isn't enough.'

'No?' Seeing the intention on his face, she backed away, only to feel the hard edge of his desk nudging the backs of her thighs.

'No, Brant, please!' Her hands flew up to stop him, but she was no match for his determination. His mouth came down on hers, silencing the plea on her lips. She moaned as he caught her against him, despairing at her own weakness, yet glorying in it too as her body recognised and responded to the hard domination of his.

'Oh, God…' The groan came from deep in his chest, and suddenly he was dragging her with him, over onto the couch.

She didn't even think about resisting him now. She couldn't think about anything but that long, lithe body pressing hers against the studded leather, the latent strength of him beneath his jacket, the burning ecstasy of his mouth on hers.

His hands had slid under her top and were moving with breath-catching expertise over the heated tautness of her ribcage, while his lips touched tortuous kisses to the long line of her throat.

'What is it you want?' Colour suffused the dark symmetry of his face, and his eyelids were heavy with desire. 'Show me.'

Annie closed her eyes, gritting her teeth against the sensations that rocked her. *Don't ask. Just touch me!* her body screamed, while consciously she fought the urge to arch her back in aching submission to his teasing hands.

'Show me.' His voice was low and sexy, chocolate-rich. Deftly, somehow, he had unfastened the small pearl buttons of her top.

Lashes pressed against the wells of her eyes, she couldn't look at him as the stretchy little garment fell open, exposing her lacy burgundy bra. She felt the heat of his gaze on her breasts above the tantalising balcony cups, the warmth of the sharp breath he exhaled, feather-light across the pale cream of her skin. 'Look at me,' he commanded.

Against her will, Annie obeyed. The hard contours of his face were etched with stark desire. With her lashes hiding the wanting in her eyes, she saw him purse his lips, blow lightly across the heated flesh of her upper breasts, the action sensuously cool, erotic. The hands that had been encircling her tiny waist slid along her ribcage to the outer edges of her breasts, stroking and teasing, sliding down again without granting the pleasure she craved.

Annie sucked in her breath, wanting to grab the hard tendons of his wrists and drag his hands up to feel their fondling warmth on her aching flesh.

'Yes?' he queried, feigning innocence.

Murmuring her frustration, not caring any more what he thought about her, she twisted her body towards him with a shuddering groan of need.

Dear heaven! she thought when he peeled back the flimsy lace, and his warm and seeking mouth closed over one turgid breast. How could she have lived believing that one day some other man could make her feel like this? How could she have fooled herself that that night with him had been no more than some casual affair? He had something that was as essential to her as earth and air, as water and sunlight. Deny it though she had, she could only admit to herself now that she had been born solely for this man's lovemaking.

Tremblingly, she clutched at the fine sleeve of his shirt, thinking she would die of ecstasy when he moulded the aching mounds to his warm palms, his slightly calloused thumbs creating a delicious friction as they played across the sensitive peaks.

Expressing her pleasure in small involuntary sobs, she brought her legs up to try and ease the need that was piercing her loins, knowing that the only thing that could do that would be his total possession of her.

'Brant...' Her hips jerked convulsively towards the hand that had slipped beneath the waistband of her jeans, warm and unbearably arousing across the flat plane of her stomach. She was drowning in desire, wanting to touch him, for him to touch her as he was doing now with that experienced hand seeking out her most secret places, to lie here naked with him, flesh against flesh...

Roughly he dragged in his breath. 'No, Annie,' he said thickly, releasing her.

Sore with disappointment, she opened her eyes, saw him battling for control.

'When we do this properly, you're going to be in my bed. As my wife. I'm afraid, darling, that nothing less will do.'

'No.' Quickly she sat up, not sure what she was rejecting most. His proposal, or his refusal to finish what he had started.

'I'm afraid so, Annie.'

'You bastard.' She couldn't stop the small invective that escaped her. Frustration seemed to be eating her insides away. He had done it deliberately, she thought, fumbling with her pearl buttons, just to see how far she'd let him go, and bitterly now she threw at him, 'You never had any such scruples before!'

A shadow seemed to flit across his face. 'Yes, well...' he breathed, grim-mouthed, not at all pleased at being reminded. 'We all change, don't we?'

'Do we?' Her smile was forced, her tone slightly acrid. Of course. She wasn't just someone to have a casual fling with any more. She had something he wanted and therefore was much more important to him now. But he hadn't said he loved her. How could he? she thought, almost laughing. Men like him didn't allow themselves to be swept off their feet by girls like her. Oh, she didn't doubt that physically he wanted her as much as she wanted him. But in other areas he would prefer the sophisticated type, like Naomi, the woman he still mourned. So how could she marry him? How could she guarantee that he wouldn't want someone more suited to him when he had grown tired of their *expedient* arrangement? Of her—as he surely would, in time? As Warren had, she thought bitterly. As they all did.

'Are you involved with someone else?' With one hand resting on the back of the couch, Brant was studying her with penetrating shrewdness, wise to the turmoil she knew showed on her face.

'Do you think I could do what I just did if I was?' she fired back incredulously, unable to help the wounded accusation that trickled through her words, that said, *Unlike a man! Unlike a man, who can just take his pleasure and then move on!*

'Then it would be just you and me, Annie,' he said. 'Just you, me and the boys. After all, it isn't our past—or our future—that's the crucial thing here, is it? It's Sean's and Jack's. I want to make their lives as trauma-free as possible in all this and I'd like to hope that you would want that too.' The leather protested softly as he moved, getting to his feet. 'Think about it,' he advised quietly. 'In the meantime...' he had moved over to the desk and was riffling through some papers, all traces of the passionate lover checked now by a will as hard as iron '...I think what you need is a change of scenery.'

'Oh?' Concern clouded the brown eyes that looked questioningly up at him. Was he going to suggest that she left after all?

'I've got a job to take care of down on the south coast,' he informed her, coming round and perching himself on the edge of the desk. 'I'll be gone for a week or two and I thought you might like to come with me. You and the boys.'

Would she? It wasn't a good idea, she decided, because even now her senses were attuned to every single aspect of him: that air of immeasurable self-confidence, his sexual charisma, the way one long leg was bent slightly so that the expensive fabric of his suit strained across his thigh. But the thought of leaving this grand mansion of a house—for however short a time—was too much to resist and, too quickly, she found herself asking, 'Where will we be staying?' She imagined the type of hotel. Five-star. Formal, but without the constant challenge to her propensity for creating chaos.

'At Brooklands.'

An Important Message from the Editors

Dear Reader,

Because you've chosen to read one of our fine romance novels, we'd like to say "thank you!" And, as a **special** way to thank you, we've selected <u>two more</u> of the books you love so well **plus** two exciting Mystery Gifts to send you — absolutely <u>FREE</u>!

Please enjoy them with our compliments...

Pam Powers

Lift here

Peel off seal and place inside...

How to validate your Editor's
"Thank You"
FREE GIFTS

1. Peel off gift seal from front cover. Place it in space provided at right. This automatically entitles you to receive 2 FREE BOOKS and 2 FREE mystery gifts.

2. Send back this card and you'll get 2 new Harlequin *Presents*® novels. These books have a cover price of $4.50 or more each in the U.S. and $5.25 or more each in Canada, but they are yours to keep absolutely free.

3. There's no catch. You're under no obligation to buy anything. We charge nothing—ZERO—for your first shipment. And you don't have to make any minimum number of purchases—not even one!

4. The fact is, thousands of readers enjoy receiving their books by mail from The Harlequin Reader Service®. They enjoy the convenience of home delivery...they like getting the best new novels at discount prices BEFORE they're available in stores... and they love their Reader to Reader subscriber newsletter featuring author news, special book offers, book reviews and much more!

5. We hope that after receiving your free books you'll want to remain a subscriber. But the choice is yours— to continue or cancel, any time at all! So why not take us up on our invitation, with no risk of any kind. You'll be glad you did!

GET TWO *Free* MYSTERY GIFTS...

*SURPRISE MYSTERY GIFTS COULD BE YOURS **FREE** AS A SPECIAL "THANK YOU" FROM THE EDITORS*

'Brooklands?' Definitely five-star.

He tossed a letter down on the desk. 'My house down there.'

Annie's hopes sank just a little. Naturally, he'd have houses all over the place, she thought. Each with its own retinue of staff, no doubt, in residence.

'Fine,' she accepted, with a careless little shrug.

They left the following morning, stopping for a refreshment break *en route*.

Brant knew of a quiet spot, which turned out to be a secluded meadow with a narrow river winding through it, reached through a stile, some way off the main road.

'You're fiercely independent, aren't you?' he remarked when they were tucking into the picnic lunch that Annie had insisted on preparing herself early that morning, spread out on the green tartan rug she usually kept in her car. She would have brought that too, if he hadn't said that there was a four-by-four sitting in the garage at Brooklands for her to use if she needed to, but she had managed to get her way when she had insisted on looking after the boys herself for however long they were away, and assured him that she didn't need a nanny.

She was sitting with her legs drawn up, giving Sean a Marmite soldier. Facing her, Brant was pouring orange juice for Jack.

The sun, warm on her arms and semi-bare legs, was making Sean's hair gleam almost red. Like Naomi's, she thought and, considering what he had said about her being independent, asked, 'Does that rankle in some way?'

'Not at all.' Briefly his eyes touched on the shapely length of her calves—exposed by the knee-length trousers—before returning to their task, his hands sure and capable even in the handling of a toddler's plastic beaker. 'It's good.'

Well, he would think that, Annie decided. A man like him wouldn't welcome a mouse of a woman for a wife and she was quite sure he wouldn't have proposed to her if she had been.

She considered what marriage to a man in Brant's position might mean. The social events. Entertaining, both in his London home and at this Brooklands place, or wherever else she might find herself with him. Having to smile at the people who would go all out to ingratiate themselves with her influential and dynamic husband—as she had seen others do in the past—and with her, just because she was married to him. Independent she might be, but such superficial friendship would make her want to turn tail and run.

'Do you like parties?' she was asking before she could stop herself.

Letting Jack toddle away from him with his freshly filled beaker, Brant frowned.

'Parties?' The white T-shirt he wore with khaki chinos pulled tautly across his shoulders as he reached for a sandwich from the tartan rug. 'Why? Are you planning one?'

She shook her head emphatically.

'I didn't think so,' he said. Unfortunately, though, her question seemed to give him licence to study her more thoroughly, especially since Sean, having had enough of his Marmite soldiers, was toddling precariously over towards Jack. She moistened her lips, feeling those shrewd eyes slide over the wild tumble of her hair, over her neutral top with its deep V-neck that was suddenly a little too deep to be decent; over her smooth hips and legs to the tips of her sandaled feet. 'You're a child of nature, Annie. I can't imagine you being too happy socialising on any grand scale, or doing anything that intruded on the simplicity of your own nature, where you weren't creating…'

'Havoc?' she supplied wryly.

His mouth twitched as she reminded him. 'I was going to say where you weren't being creative, letting your natural talents develop. For a girl like you, I would imagine the so-called good life would pale very quickly.'

'Oh,' was all she could say in response. She supposed that was a compliment of sorts, and so close to what she had been thinking a few moments ago that imperceptibly she shivered. It did, however, give her an insight into Brant's enigmatic and, she guessed, very complex character, because if he was discerning enough to recognise those things in her, surely he would feel the same way too?

Hearing the childish laughter, Annie glanced over her shoulder. Jack and Sean were tearing up daisies, throwing them at each other. They were getting along well, she thought. Behind them, some distance away, the silent river flowed towards a neighbouring village. She imagined its small stone houses, like others they had passed, basking in the afternoon sun. She could see the spire of its church peeping above the trees, heard the lowing of a cow some-where in one of the adjoining fields, and felt the breeze lift her hair, carrying with it the sweet, evocative scent of wild honeysuckle.

'Have you brought anyone else here?' It was out before she could stop herself, but it was something she had been wondering ever since they had arrived.

'Yes.'

She wished then that she hadn't asked.

'My father,' he clarified. 'Or rather…he brought me. We had a fishing holiday. Over in Briarsfield there.' This with a jerk of his chin towards the village that Annie had been visualising. 'Coarse fish,' he went on. 'The type you toss back and watch swim away with hopefully not much more than their pride hurt.' She was glad he'd told her that. 'I must have been nine or ten.'

Try though she did, she couldn't picture him as a child.

'It was the last holiday we had together. He died the following year.'

'I'm sorry.'

'It was a long time ago,' he said.

'Someone said he was a steeplejack.' She couldn't remember who had told her that, even if it was right.

'Does that surprise you?' He had picked up on the uncertainty in her voice. 'Hard-hewn and very down-to-earth and I learned a hell of a lot from him. And you're thinking why on earth did a cultured pearl like my mother get herself involved with a rough diamond from such a totally different background from her own?'

'Well, I...' She supposed she was.

'So did her family,' Brant went on, 'which was why they disowned her totally when she went against their wishes and married him. When he died so young, one would think they would have helped her, but they didn't. He had an accident. At work.' She remembered being told that too. 'And we were left to fend for ourselves.'

But he had shown them, Annie thought. He wasn't saying that. Maybe he wasn't even thinking it, but he had.

Now she knew what drove him, she could understand him more. He was a complex blend of two cultures that between them had produced the multi-faceted sophisticate. The raw-edged youth had ground down the rougher edges of his persona to emerge as the urbane yet uncompromising character he was today.

As she realized just how much strength of will and determination such a progress would have taken, a little shudder ran through Annie. He fascinated and intrigued her, excited and scared her.

Even so, he was great with the children. Lying back on the rug after they had eaten, the warm sun caressing her face and limbs, she listened to Jack's and Sean's delighted squeals as Brant treated them to piggyback rides in turn.

Through the screen of her lashes, her hands behind her head, covertly she watched the big man at play. He was racing round the field, bouncing Jack on his shoulders, while Sean followed, hooting like a train, behind them. Both boys were having the time of their lives. Listening to Jack's ecstatic shrieks as he clung to Brant's lithe frame, Annie sensed that the little boy hadn't had too much of this. That though Brant tried to be there for him, the very nature of his work demanded that for a lot of the time he had to be somewhere else. As Felicity had nowhere near the same amount of energy to play with the child, and without a mother, Annie guessed that Jack must have missed out on a great deal.

A bee droned lazily past her ear, a soporific sound over Sean's sudden demands that it was his turn.

Likewise Sean, suddenly Annie found herself thinking. She had tried to give him all that a mother could give her child. Love. A comfortable and secure home. Time. But she had to work to provide for them both and sometimes her work demanded far more than she wanted to give. Sometimes she was tired, and because of that, because of her single-motherhood, she realised that Sean was missing out, too.

Being in her position had its advantages. It might even be ideal for some people. But it took two—a man and a woman, with a balance of ideas and opinions, working together and complementing each other, to provide the best possible upbringing for a child.

'For the boys' sake,' Brant had said. ''It's their future that matters.'' So was she being selfish even hesitating over his proposal? Was she being foolish and impractical telling herself that the only thing stopping her was a lack of any real feeling for her on Brant's part? Could they build a home for both boys only on the devastating sexual chemistry that flared between them? Because there was no doubt that, in that department at least, Brant Cadman wanted her as desperately, if it was possible, as she wanted him.

* * *

They arrived at Brooklands some time during the afternoon.

What Annie had been expecting as Brant brought the Mercedes off the main highway to follow a steep, narrow road down into a valley, she wasn't sure. But as they passed through the sleepy Dorset village nestling under the chalk downland and Brant drew up alongside a building on the very fringes of the village, she realised that nothing could have been further from her mind.

The house, which looked as though it had once been several cottages, had been converted into one property. The mid-afternoon sun spilled a golden wash over its mellow stone walls, drawing a rich fragrance from a pale peach climbing rose which was cascading over the wrought-iron curlicues of the porch. Several of the small-paned windows were open, letting in the warmth, Annie appreciated, stepping out of the car, noticing with a satisfied pleasure the white lacy curtains stirring in the gentle breeze.

But it was the silence that met them after the wearing roar of traffic on the busy highway, and now that Brant had turned off the car's engine, that impressed her most. There was no sound, nothing but the mellifluous notes of a thrush somewhere in the high hedgerow, and the rush of a stream tumbling alongside the house between its low boundary wall and the grassy verge that gave on to the country road.

Brant was smiling at her surprised pleasure. 'Welcome to Brooklands,' he said.

Carrying Sean, while Brant took charge of Jack, Annie allowed him to guide them into the house.

The same rustic simplicity was reflected inside, she discovered, captivated by its many original features. By its traditional oak beams, and flagstone floors, its surprisingly open spaces and cosy nooks. The whole place was an amalgam of charm and character, she decided, from the wide, country kitchen with its free-standing oak cabinets and dresser, which she glimpsed off to the left on her way in, to the log-stacked inglenook fireplace and crooked walls of the spacious sitting room they had just entered.

Here comfort and relaxation seemed to take precedence in the soft sofas and chairs with their plump loose cushions and simple throws, in the shelves full of books, in tapestries and in the colourfully-spun rugs that followed the rest of the décor with their natural tones.

Brant was releasing Jack, who, hearing a familiar voice, now rushed over and threw his arms around the stout, matronly legs of the woman coming through the doorway.

The three adults laughed, and Brant carried out the introductions.

Connie Vexx looked anything but what her name suggested, Annie decided. With only a few strands of grey streaking her brown hair, plump and rosy-cheeked, she epitomised the easy-going countrywoman in her flowery sundress and serviceable sandals. Annie smiled as she listened to what Brant was telling her.

Connie, apparently a widow, lived in the village with her nephew and three dogs and had looked after the cottage for twelve years for the previous owner. 'When I took it over, Connie came as part of the package,' he quipped in conclusion, the smile that blazed through that statement assuring Annie of the depth of affection he obviously held for his housekeeper.

'I'll take the little one,' Connie offered generously, since Sean, who was fretting for his freedom, seemed to be getting heavier by the second. Then, clutching a tiny hand in the capable plumpness of each of her own, she said, 'I'll make some tea. If you'd like to get yourselves comfortable, I'll take these two into the kitchen. I've made just the thing for you two little men to nibble.'

As she padded away, chatting easily to the children, Annie marvelled at how readily the boys took to her.

Connie Vexx, like this house, Annie decided, looking

around her, embodied warmth and comfort and simplicity. Even the garden, she thought, with her gaze travelling to the open window, reflected the same charm and simplicity in its ancient hedges of dark green yew, its wild beds of lavender—whose scent was drifting in and mingling with the delicious aroma of home-made bread and yeasty cakes; in the bright, riotous beds of poppy and colourful snapdragons, and the black-eyed, magenta blooms she couldn't even name.

She didn't realise how transparent her surprised pleasure was until Brant spoke.

'What were you expecting?' he probed softly.

She looked up at him, felt a little *frisson* run through her at suddenly finding herself alone with him. 'I don't know. I—'

'Didn't you see me as a country buff at heart?'

Well, she hadn't, had she? She had imagined him to be a creature of contemporary luxury, signified by his awesome London home. But here there were no formal brocades that could be soiled by sticky substances, no walls that couldn't be scrubbed clean of a lost acrylic taken by tiny, investigative hands.

A change of scenery, he had said after she had bemoaned the fact that she couldn't work, but there would be nothing, she thought, to stop her here. Had he known that? Was that why he had brought her here? Or was it solely for his peace of mind, knowing that here in these friendlier, more rustic surroundings she would be unlikely to do very much damage?

'I bought this place eighteen months ago,' he said, strolling over to the window, and with a sigh of obvious satisfaction stood with his hands in the back pockets of his chinos, looking out.

Greedily, Annie's gaze roamed freely over the long, lean length of him, eyes devouring every sinew of his hair-furred arms, the latent strength of muscle beneath the T-shirt that moulded itself to his broad back, the hard, firm cage of his hips.

'I needed somewhere where I could unwind,' he told her. 'To be alone with Jack.'

So Naomi had never been there, Annie calculated, her brain suddenly kicking into gear. She couldn't have, if he had only bought the place eighteen months ago, she realised, and derived a secret comfort in knowing that.

CHAPTER SEVEN

IT WAS a spell of glorious weather, which began with a mellow gentleness and then blazed into the fierce, golden heat of high summer.

The county was packed with tourists, so that between their vividly striped deckchairs and windbreaks, and the bright stalls selling their colourful beach wares, there was scarcely a glimpse of pale sand left visible on the popular Weymouth Bay.

It was, however, the blend of Jurassic limestone with the more spectacular vertical white chalk cliffs that fired Annie's imagination, the reds and yellow clays of the rocks and the deserted sand and shingle beaches further along the coast—where no path allowed any public access—offering only a wild remoteness that filled her with awe and inspiration.

'It's timeless and unchallenged,' Brant told her one day when they were out walking the coastal path above the famous Durdle Door, a magnificent arch of rock projecting into the azure sea. 'It was here long before we were, and will be here long, long after we've gone.'

Silently Annie agreed, only able to nod from the breathtaking scenery that nature had carved out of the centuries. It was all she had needed—this change, the cottage—because since coming here over a week ago, away from the oppressive formality and ghosts of Brant's London home, her creative juices had not only started flowing again, but also returned in force. She had come out today to take some photographs, eager for a new picture, a different subject to paint, and as it was the weekend, and Brant wasn't working,

Connie had suggested that she and her nephew take the boys to a donkey sanctuary so that Brant could accompany her.

The camera shutter clicked, catching him looking like some brooding god of the rocks against the long and rugged backdrop of the coast.

'Got ya!' Annie proclaimed, laughing at his total surprise.

'You little vixen! You're incorrigible with that camera. Don't you dare!' he warned, his hand shielding his face from the sun as she pointed it at him again. But her finger was already depressing the button, and, seeing the sudden promise of retribution on his face, she gave a small shriek and darted away.

She didn't get very far. He was much too quick for her for one thing. For another, the toe of her sandal caught in a rut in the grassy hillside and she tumbled, uttering an excited little scream, not so much from the fall, but from the strong hands that were pulling her round before he came down on top of her.

'So who's got who now?' He was laughing now that he could see she wasn't hurt, pinning her arms mercilessly above her head.

Shaken, breathless, and only because of the stirring weight of him pressing into her, all she could think of to say was, 'My camera!'

'Your camera's fine.' Capturing her wrists in his large hand, he reached just above her shoulder and picked it up, proving it to her. 'So what are you planning to do? Make me the next subject of that beautiful imagination?'

She gave a tremulous little laugh. 'You flatter yourself!'

'Do I?' His laughter was warm against her cheek and she groaned as his hips ground suggestively into hers. 'Well, just in case, let me give you a little bit extra to go on.'

She couldn't stop the mouth that was swooping to take hers. Nor did she want to, the hands that he was suddenly releasing sliding eagerly around him, her body arching in absolute surrender to his.

He was as rugged as the cliffs above which they were lying—as hard and untameable. And she wanted him! she thought, shuddering from the depth of her need, showing him by lifting her hips to meet his hard arousal while his lips burned kisses along her jaw, her throat, the scented valley of her breasts above her clinging sun-top...

'This isn't wise,' he rasped, rolling away from her. 'Not unless you agree to marry me.'

So he was still insisting on that.

Sucking in her breath, Annie followed his example and sat up.

'Shouldn't that be my line?' she said with a nervous little laugh, stalling for time. She couldn't—wouldn't just rush into a marriage—not a second time.

Impatiently, he said, 'You know what I mean.' He wasn't a man used to waiting for anything. 'There are important issues at stake. Life-changing issues. We need to know where we're headed so we can get on with our lives.'

He had said a similar thing that morning, when the letter had arrived. The letter that informed her, without any doubt, that Sean was his. His and Naomi's. Annie had already known what the DNA test would reveal. Deep down, she imagined, they both had. It was just that confirmation of it only cemented Brant's claim on the little boy.

'There *is* only one solution, Annie,' he had stressed as she stood in the cottage garden, taking steadying breaths, listening achingly to her child's chuckles through the open window of the kitchen, where Connie, aware of the situation and the seriousness of the letter, was, at that moment, keeping both boys amused. 'My way there's no need for either of us to give either child up. But I'm sure you can appreciate that I want Sean as much as you do.'

And he would have him—fight for custody of him, if he

had to, Annie thought now, with an almost painful tightening of her stomach, tearing absently at the coarse grass. He hadn't actually said that, but his tone had implied it. He loved Jack, but Sean was a part of the woman he had married, as well as his rightful son and heir, and blood would mean everything, she suspected, to a man like Brant.

'You want to switch them back, don't you?' She couldn't look at him as she asked it, the question seeming to stab her in the chest.

There was some movement a little way above them, voices, a young man and woman, walking a dog along the coastal path.

'No,' Brant said heavily, glancing up at the couple. They were holding hands, looking contented, happy. 'That's what I want to avoid.'

'But you will. If I don't...do what you're asking. In the end, you will, won't you?'

She caught his sudden sharp intake of breath before he stood up, brushing grass off his chinos.

'Who knows what any of us will do—as you put it,' he said with undisguised scorn, 'in the end?'

Over the next few days, a barrier seemed to erect itself between them. A tension, which sprang not only from Annie's reluctance to commit herself, but also from an increasingly heightened awareness of each other. In the casual, relaxed atmosphere of the cottage, that mutual chemistry that had been hard enough to ignore back in the larger, formal house seemed now to charge the air with something electric every time they found themselves in the same room.

While he was out, however, giving hands-on advice on the new leisure complex his company was developing along the coast, and with Connie always eager to take the boys off her hands, Annie managed to complete two miniature paintings. One was a pale vase of blood-red poppies with the kitchen window as a backdrop, the other, drawn from memory, a cheeky blue-tit she had watched drinking from an old dripping pipe that jutted out under the low eaves of the house.

She had had her photographs developed in Weymouth, driving down there in the four-by-four and bringing them back one day when everyone was out. Racing up to her bedroom and flopping down on the chintzy coverlet of the big brass bed, she pulled them out of their sleeve, searching almost furtively for the ones she had taken of Brant.

There he was in profile, the sweep of his brow, with that prominent nose and jaw etching him as ruthless as the sea that had carved its will into the cliffs and formed the numerous red bays and hazy headlands behind him.

She was painting in the garden, fast and freely on her water-colour pad under the sun-umbrella and wasn't aware that anyone was back until Brant asked over her shoulder, 'Is that how you see me?'

Annie almost dropped her brush. She hadn't been expecting him for hours!

'It's…interesting,' he commented, mouth twitching as he tilted his head to study the water-colour.

'I just thought I'd try some portraiture,' she lied with her tongue seeming to cleave to her mouth, because it was much more than that.

What she had unleashed through her brush was the yearning of her own sexuality, bold splashes of colour, applied with a wide, sheer-edged brush, creating a creature more barbaric-looking than the dark-suited man who was standing, with his hand on the table, leaning over her. This one showed a Brant whose fullness of mouth suggested a powerful lust, the uncompromising lines of his body pulsating with raw sensuality.

'I see,' he said, and he did if the wealth of meaning in those two words was anything to go by.

'No, you don't,' she argued pointlessly, and made the mistake of glancing up at him, only to find herself caught in the hot snare of his gaze.

A dangerous heat flooded through. He hadn't moved and the heady spice of his cologne was playing a dangerous game with her senses, overriding the scent of lavender from a bright bed beside her chair.

'I've always wondered if you weren't expressing yourself through the wrong medium.'

Annie frowned, unable to stop looking into those beautiful irises. 'Come again?' she breathed, with a prickly heat tingling down her spine.

'I remember seeing some of your designs when you worked for my company. They were...' his hand indicated the painting '...big and bold and striking. You've got a wild, abandoned nature, Annie. Maybe your soul's screaming to be looser. Freer. Ever thought about that?'

Annie swallowed, disconcerted by his description of her. What was he doing? Psychoanalysing her now?

Having watched a butterfly settle on one of the purple flags of lavender, she turned back to him with her eyes wary, guarded. 'What are you saying exactly?'

'What I'm saying,' he started to clarify, straightening so that she could breathe again, 'is that somehow it doesn't seem altogether in character constraining that wild streak of yours within the disciplined framework of the miniature. As though you're afraid to stray from within its safe, secure perimeters...'

'I most certainly am not!'

'You're straying beyond them now. That fiery retort doesn't spring from a nature constrained by limits or rigid discipline. Fire goes its own way, dominating anything and everything except what's equipped to control it.'

His words made Annie's throat contract with need, and fear induced by that need. He wasn't just talking about the limitations of her painting. He was alluding to the two of them, and that blazing attraction between them.

'I've done larger, looser paintings in my time,' she breathed, pretending his hidden meaning had gone entirely over her head. 'But big isn't necessarily better!' she snapped, as a deliberate dig at him, and could have kicked herself for the way his eyebrow lifted in mocking scepticism.

'When was that?' he asked roughly, all amusement gone now. 'Before Maddox broke your spirit?'

How dared he? 'No one broke my spirit!'

'All right, then. Caged it up.'

'No one caged it up. And leave Warren out of this,' she advised thickly. 'He's nothing to do with my painting.'

'Just with every other aspect of what's happened—what happens—in your life!'

Was he? Annie wondered suddenly. She'd never thought so. So what aspects was Brant referring to? Her reluctance to marry him? To let herself fall victim to the power of her emotions for a second time with yet another man who didn't love her? 'Well, what do you expect?' she tossed up at him. 'Being thrown over for somebody else two weeks before my wedding wasn't exactly a bundle of laughs!'

'I appreciate that,' he breathed, with something like understanding darkening his eyes. 'Nor is being left to cope alone with a child. But all men aren't the same, Annie. You were just unlucky—and if you'd only let those defences down for a while, give me the chance—I'd prove it to you.'

He was walking away, leaving her gazing wonderingly after him as he strode back towards the house.

Things weren't made any easier when Jack went down with a cold. For a couple of days he was feverish and grizzling, during which time the weather turned oppressively hot.

Brant's personal involvement with the leisure-centre development meant a few late meetings and so, left on her own one evening, hot and sticky and having had a gruelling day with Jack, Annie settled both boys down early, had a long, leisurely bath, then took herself off to bed with a paperback novel.

Her window was open, but there wasn't a hint of a breeze to cool the room. The perfume of night-scented stocks was heavy on the air. By the time she switched off her lamp, Brant still wasn't home.

Lying there in the darkness, with just a cool cotton sheet covering her, she listened for his car above the tumbling of the stream, restless in its eternal quest for the sea on the other side of the valley behind the limestone hills. Eventually, the sound lulled her to sleep.

It was the lightning that woke her, and the rain being tossed against the small window like handfuls of shingle.

Then she heard it. The sound of one of the boys crying.

Throwing back the sheet, wearing only her thin slip of a nightdress, Annie padded barefoot onto the landing. It was Jack, ever the lighter sleeper of the two.

The thunder must have frightened him, she thought, hurrying into his bedroom. The cries coming from the little cotbed were broken and snuffly.

Another flash of lightning lit the night sky, illuminating Jack's room and the figure of Brant in a dark towelling robe coming through the opposite doorway that led onto a higher landing and his own room.

'I heard him crying,' Annie whispered, reaching his bed at the same time as Brant. He was already switching on the tiny lamp.

Jack was sitting up now, blinking from the light, tears streaming down his face as he looked from one to the other on opposing sides of his bed.

'It's all right, Jack.' They whispered it simultaneously just as a crash of thunder overhead seemed to rock the house.

Jack's wails were suddenly heart-rending, and quickly Annie stooped to pick him up. It was to Brant, however, that the little boy lifted his arms for reassurance and in total trust.

Well, of course it was, Annie tried to reason. After all, Brant was the only parent Jack had ever known. But her arms ached with the need to comfort what was, after all, her own child. Never had she felt it as acutely as now, when fulfilment of that need was being so naturally, yet so cruelly, denied her.

Brant was rocking him, whispering coaxing words. 'Hush, Jack. You'll wake Sean. And we won't want that, will we?'

Across the landing, Sean was apparently sleeping soundly, but Jack's screams were getting louder, his little lungs contesting with the thunder and the lashing rain.

'Let me,' Annie pleaded, coming round to Brant's side, unable to bear it any longer.

For a moment Brant seemed hesitant. Jack had wanted his father, after all. After a moment, though, he handed the boy over, his hand accidentally brushing her breast as he placed the toddler into her outstretched arms.

'He's hot,' Brant said. 'And flushed.'

'He'll be all right.' Holding Jack close, she sat down on the chair beside the bed, palming his feverish little brow.

'It's that damn cold. Perhaps I should ring the doctor.'

'He'll be OK. He's just worked up.' Glancing at Brant, she thought she had never seen him so nonplussed, concerned. 'Trust me,' she breathed reassuringly, and with a mother's instinct for what was right.

With her lips against the soft dark mop of Jack's hair, she started to murmur soothing little phrases, stroking his forehead, rocking him all the while. He was hot—yes—and a bit congested, but already his cries were beginning to subside.

Maybe it was all down to scent, or chemistry, or both, Annie thought when the child's sobs had turned to nothing more than little whimpers of discomfort, but Jack, she was certain, sensed a bond as strong as any infant's for its mother.

A fierce clutch of maternal possession almost took her breath away and in that instant she knew that she could never let him go.

There had been a storm the night that he was born. It had caused a power failure and it had been a few precious minutes before the hospital generator had been up and running, throwing the place into chaos. That was what the authority dealing with the investigation had since offered as the only explanation for the mix-up.

Brant had had other, more pressing things to worry about in Naomi's condition to recall the storm. But Annie did. She remembered thinking how the thunder and driving rain beyond the hospital window had seemed to enclose her and her newborn son in their own little world; recalled vividly how the tiny bundle in her arms had seemed to make up for all the heartache and humiliation she had previously suffered. Silently she had vowed to give him everything to make up for any lack of paternal love.

Even now she could hear his little cries as a nurse had carried him away, only seconds before the lights went out in her room, in the corridor, outside in the street. She had lain there in the darkness, worrying that he might be frightened, or instinctively missing the sound and scent and tangible comfort of his mother. She couldn't forget how she had ached for the return of her son.

When they brought him back he had been subdued and sleepy, only crying lustily when she couldn't fulfil his hungry demands to be fed. But it hadn't been her baby, because they had given hers to someone else. To a man who, ironically, she had spent one glorious night with, and whose wife had just happened to give birth on exactly the same day as herself.

Feet planted slightly apart, Brant was looking down at her sitting there cushioning the now sleepy dark head against her shoulder.

'I can't give him up, Annie.' Disconcertingly, it was as if he had read her mind, recognised the possessive emotions burning inside her. 'He's been with me from the beginning—kept me going through all the sleepless nights, the soul-searching and the guilt when I couldn't stop blaming myself...'

Blaming himself? Annie queried silently, listening to Jack's steady, if rather snuffled, breathing, knowing without Brant having to spell it out that he was referring to what had happened to Naomi.

The subdued light from the lamp slashed harsh shadows across a face already scored by some deep, inner struggle and Annie felt pain spear her somewhere around the area of her heart.

'It wasn't your fault,' she whispered in a voice shaky with emotion, realising that some men might have blamed the child for what had happened. The history books were full of it. It wasn't easy, though, being reminded of how much Naomi had meant to him.

'No.' He breathed a long sigh, sounding unconvinced. 'But then you don't share my demons, do you? Nor do you have someone else's memory to respect—to consider in all this...' He drew another ragged breath. 'You don't have the monopoly on feelings, Annie. Don't you think it's as hard for me—harder, if that's possible—as it is for you? Losing a wife in childbirth and to be told that the child she died giving birth to—a child she never even held—was just given away...' Pained incredulity cracked his voice, giving her a glimpse of how keenly it must have affected him when he had first been told, although she had thought about it—and often. 'But just like you with Sean…' a contemplative smile couldn't hide the anguish lining his face as he studied the sleeping infant in her arms '…I know every laugh. Every tear. Every mood, right down to his last tantrum. Do you think I could just hand him over—after bringing him up for two years believing he was my son?'

The sharp edge of his pain sliced through her emotions, breaking through her own pain, her doubts, her fear.

If someone could tell her that this nightmare had never started, that it was all a mistake and that the child she believed was hers was still hers and not some other woman's… Annie sucked in her breath from the depth of her wanting. Wouldn't she welcome that? If she could have Sean and little Jack, knowing that one was as much hers as the other, wouldn't she move heaven and earth to make it possible?

The thunder came now as only a faint rumble in the distance. The rain too had eased. Only the stream, swollen from the storm, danced and bubbled with its clear, eternal song alongside the cottage.

Like voices in turmoil, Annie thought absently. Timeless, dependable voices. Voices of truth.

Lifting her face to Brant's, tremulously she whispered, 'He is your son.'

CHAPTER EIGHT

ONLY the stream and the quiet tick of the clock on Jack's chest of drawers broke the silence that seemed to stretch away into eternity.

'What are you saying?' Brant whispered hoarsely.

'He's yours,' Annie reiterated. 'Not Warren's as you were so quick to assume.'

'But...' So many emotions chased across his face. Shock. Confusion. Bewilderment. 'How can he be? We took precautions. You told me you were on the Pill...' The cleft between his eyebrows deepened. 'And the boys were born on the same day. Oh, I know Naomi had a long and difficult pregnancy and that Sean was born later than expected, but he was conceived at least...' he made a sharp movement with his head, trying to jolt his brain into clarity '...five weeks before we...' His sentence tailed off. She could see him grappling with his thoughts. 'Unless Jack was born prematurely—' He broke off again, seeing Annie's silent negation.

'About three weeks early, but not premature,' she told him. In fact, when she had been worrying about her baby coming earlier than had been estimated, the doctor had assured her that anything between thirty-seven and forty-two weeks was considered a normal, healthy birth. She had obviously been at one end of the spectrum while Naomi, presumably, had been at the other. Brant had said five weeks. But how could he have been so sure?

'Are you saying then that not only did a condom fail, but also that the Pill didn't work either?' He sounded as though he didn't believe her—and who could blame him? she thought.

'I know, unbelievable really, isn't it?' Did she sound bitter? Hurt? She didn't intend to, but from the way his mouth compressed that was how he had interpreted it. As if his child had been the last thing she had wanted. 'But I'd been on a course of antibiotics for a chest infection and the doctor said it had a negative effect on the Pill. Maybe the condom seeped, I don't know. But I never made love with Warren. He was obsessed about my not having babies at that stage of his career. He was obsessive about my taking the Pill. Maybe I didn't feel enough for him physically as I should have, but when I did start taking it, it was only a few weeks to go till our wedding, and as we hadn't made love I decided I wanted to wait until we were married. A real fairy-tale wedding, or so I thought. When he agreed so readily, I didn't realise it was because he was already having it off with someone else! But I was a virgin until we—until you and I...' She almost choked on her words, the bitterness of abandonment—of being tossed aside as second best—evident in her voice. But it was Brant's indifference to her that hurt most—not Warren's.

Brant's face was criss-crossed by surprise and bewilderment. 'It wasn't apparent,' he breathed.

She shrugged. 'Well, no. It happens, I'm told.'

'Why didn't you tell me?' The dark robe gaped, exposing a good deal of chest hair as he slipped his hands into his pockets. He looked hurt, baffled, betrayed. 'Why have you waited until now?'

'I don't know. I—'

'Why, Annie?' There was a ragged edge to his voice.

'I was afraid.'

'Of what?'

'I don't know. Everything. Losing Sean—and Jack as well.'

'How?' he queried, his eyes narrowing in contemplation.

She didn't answer, but then it didn't take much working out, she thought. Finding out Jack was his child too put him in a far stronger position than her. He could probably fight for custody of Sean if he wanted to—if she refused to hand him over—and still have access to Jack. He could control Sean's upbringing and have a say in Jack's—which he would obviously always want—and she couldn't see herself being able to do very much about it. Unless she did as he had suggested and married him...

'I should have guessed,' he was saying. 'Realised. Sometimes there were times when I couldn't get over how alike they seemed...' He looked as though he could kick himself for not realising. 'Why didn't you tell me before?' He stood with his feet planted like a giant tree, resolute, unbending. 'When you first found out?'

'What would you have done, Brant?' She gave a bitter little laugh. 'With two of us laying claim to you? Anyway, I didn't know until I came back from France, and then you were already married.'

The short, sharp breath he inhaled expressed—what? Regret at the futility of his question? 'Yes, well...' He made a movement with his arm, another futile gesture.

Had you planned to marry her? Did you only do it because she was pregnant? she wanted to ask, but the questions died in her throat. They would have been even more pointless than his had been. In the lamplight she could see all too clearly the anguish caused by talking about his marriage and the woman whose life had been so brutally cut short, and she looked down at Jack, stifling a low groan of despair.

'Perhaps you'd give me the opportunity of doing the right thing now.'

He was sacrificing his freedom in asking her. So why did she feel as though the sacrifice would be all on her part?

'But is it right?' she asked, holding Jack's warm body to her like a shield against the inevitable. 'Marrying without love?'

He seemed to need to draw breath before answering and his face was a cold, implacable mask. Perhaps, she thought, he harboured reservations too.

'I'm sure we've enough love for the boys to make up for any we might lack between ourselves,' he stated crisply, unable to guess how much that cold, unemotional statement hurt. 'And a marriage without romance—or love, as you call it—can have its compensations.'

'Like what?' she uttered tremulously.

'You aren't likely to be disillusioned or fall out of love, for one thing. And for another, you're very unlikely to get hurt.'

Annie looked at him askance. Had he been hurt at some time? Since Naomi perhaps? By Naomi?

She shook both notions away as Jack coughed suddenly, stirring restlessly in her arms.

Lifting him up, she laid her cheek against his, breathing an almost inaudible sigh of resignation. But it wasn't just Brant's relentless persuasion that had worn her down. Her future had been decided, she knew now, when she had been trying to console Jack at the height of the storm. She had lost him to a storm before, and silently this time she had promised herself—and him—with everything in her that was maternal that she would never do it again.

It was all there in her face, the love, the need and the defeat.

As he stood there, watching her, with his hands still in his pockets, Brant's chest lifted and fell in a kind of weary victory.

'We really don't have any choice, do we?' he said.

They were married two weeks later during a small civil ceremony, with only Felicity and Katrina as witnesses, and which was nothing like the big day she had been planning the first time. It was as though Brant had guessed at the doubts she still harboured and had wanted to make her his wife before she could change her mind, Annie thought, dizzy from the speed with which it had all happened.

'My, my! He's certainly a fast worker!' Katrina had remarked at the small reception held at Brant's London residence afterwards. 'Although it's about time he made it legal.' And then in answer to Annie's curious look, she had said meaningfully, 'Oh come on! Do you think I didn't *know*? Oh, I know you said you'd got pregnant because you'd had a fling with someone, and I didn't ask any questions at the time because I knew you didn't want me to, but Jack's his, isn't he?'

Startled, Annie could only nod. 'I didn't have an affair with him,' she suddenly felt the need to let Katrina know, but her friend waved her explanation aside.

'I know that. You're not the type to go stealing another woman's man.'

Well, that's something, Annie had thought, relieved. 'And it wasn't really a question of making it legal on his part. He'd already asked me to marry him before he found out about Jack.'

'I'm not surprised,' Katrina had said. 'He can't keep his eyes or his hands off you.' Over the top of her champagne glass, she directed a glance at the charismatic man across the room. In dark tailored trousers and a dark green velvet jacket setting off his wide shoulders and contrasting superbly with an immaculate white shirt and snowy carnation, he was talking to Felicity and Elise. The au pair's head was held a little too high, mouth sulky from her obvious disappointment over Brant's sudden marriage, yet still her body was held provocatively towards his. Notice me, it said. But he didn't, turning at that moment to look at Annie, and with such a feral glint in his eyes, not even an outsider could fail to notice the passions that rode him. 'Lucky girl,' Katrina breathed.

Annie looked at her friend obliquely. There was an unmistakable flush beneath the foundation the woman had used to conceal her abundant freckles. 'I thought you didn't like him.'

Katrina pulled a face. 'Anyone can change their mind, can't they?'

Sitting in the Mercedes now, with her dynamic new husband beside her, Annie mused over the way he had charmed the indomitable Katrina—as he could charm everyone—over the past couple of weeks: carrying a set of designs up to the top floor for her one day when he had been there, raising her prestige among her colleagues. Personally praising her designs for the logo on the new teen range of sportswear. Taking a look at her car when he had driven Annie over to see her one evening because it was causing her problems, and fixing it on the spot.

'Make him happy,' her mother-in-law had whispered rather seriously, kissing Annie lightly on each cheek before they had left, and now, with her breath seeming to lock in her lungs as she stole a glance at the intriguing man she had married, Annie prayed fervently that she could fulfil that requirement.

They had returned to London the day after she had accepted his proposal, having stayed in Dorset just over two weeks, and between making arrangements for the forthcoming wedding and Brant having to work, they seemed to have had very little time for each other, until now.

Wise, almost, to everything she was thinking, following a long, straight stretch of road, he suddenly reached across for her hand, saying, 'Well, here we are. Alone at last. Did you enjoy your day...Mrs Cadman?'

He liked saying that. She could tell from the proprietary way he stressed it.

'Yes,' she murmured, tingling with anticipation from the accidental brush of his hand against her tummy when he had reached across for hers. 'But I wish Mum and Dad could have been there.'

She had rung them on her return from Dorset, to let them know that she and Brant were getting married. Jane Talbot had been convinced that her daughter was pregnant and, having been assured that she wasn't, let Annie know how hurt she was that she wasn't waiting until Simon Talbot was strong enough to undertake the journey to be with them, silently reminding Annie that this was twice that they had been cheated out of a wedding, as her mother went on to tell her that her father was very upset.

He wasn't, though. Having spoken to Brant, he had made it easy for his daughter, as he always did, Annie thought fondly: congratulating her, telling her that getting married was a personal thing and that too much time and money was spent on it nowadays, and that if he could have his time over again he would do it in exactly the same way.

'Don't worry.' Brant smiled at her now, squeezing her hand reassuringly in his before releasing it to negotiate a roundabout. 'We'll get them over here soon to celebrate with us, I promise.'

They had left the boys in the care of Felicity and Elise so that they could enjoy the short break alone together, which was as much as Annie would allow herself to take.

'Your tastes are very simple,' she recalled Brant commenting with some amusement after he had offered her the choice of virtually anywhere in the world for her honeymoon and she had opted for a few days back at the cottage. But she didn't want to be too far from either of her babies and from where she might not be able to return at a moment's notice.

'Isn't that why you're marrying me?' she had joked. But now, as they turned off the main carriageway, taking the splendid Roman road towards the coast, Annie couldn't help wondering why he had married her, a man with everything, who could have had anyone. Was it really simply for their children's sake? And because he knew that they would be compatible in bed?

Surely a man like him wouldn't tie himself to a woman without feeling *something* for her, would he? she argued with herself hopefully. Yet he hadn't once told her that he cared. But was it possible that he did, and was afraid to commit himself emotionally? Afraid of looking foolish because, after all, she hadn't actually told him, had she? No, she thought, it had all been so quick that they had scarcely had time to get to know each other, and she suspected that it would take a hard-headed male like Brant much longer than the short time they had spent together to admit to caring about a woman. It was up to her, therefore, to bring those emotions—if they existed—into fruition.

'Do you think the boys will be all right for four or five days with neither of us around?' she asked worriedly, substituting one anxiety, now decidedly resolved, for another. 'Jack's used to you not being there for days at a time, but I've always been there for Sean. Supposing he needs me?'

'Then Mother will ring me immediately. Relax.' His smile was so indulgent and understanding, she could only respond with a rather sheepish one in return.

'I'm sorry.' She shrugged. 'Maternal instinct, I guess. It's hard thinking of anything else when I'm away from him.'

'Then I'm going to have to do something about that, aren't I?' he said and with such a sensual promise in his voice that a dart of excitement quivered along Annie's veins.

* * *

The early-August afternoon was turning into evening by the time they reached Brooklands, the familiar silence, broken only by the stream and the sudden protest of a startled black-bird as it took off over the old yew hedge surprising Annie as it always did.

'No,' Brant said, when she made to step inside, and with one fluid movement, lifted her up, carrying her over the threshold.

She laughed, a light, tremulous sound as she wound her arms around him, felt the soft sensuality of the jacket he had shrugged into as he'd got out of the car.

She wondered why he'd waited until now, and not carried her into the home he had shared with Naomi after they had gone back there after the ceremony. But perhaps that was why, she decided, quickly discarding the thought, because she preferred it this way anyway.

'Put me down,' she whispered, giggling, oddly embarrassed. 'Connie might be here.'

His deep laughter echoed hers. 'Connie wouldn't be that imprudent.'

Kicking the door closed behind them, he kissed her then, long and thoroughly, crushing the fine, feminine folds of her skirt against his hard body.

It was the one she had been married in, a tiered, gypsy-styled skirt in light Indian cotton, patterned in soft greens and gold. Her neutral, broderie-anglaise camisole had extended the gypsy look, her only adornment the minimal spray of soft flowers decorating her neutral floppy hat which matched the small bouquet she had carried—both of which she had left behind in London—and the gold and emerald stud earrings Brant had bought her two weeks ago to celebrate their betrothal, which she had said she preferred to an engagement ring.

'My beautiful Bohemian,' he whispered—just as he had when he had first seen her at the house that morning—easing her slowly down the length of his body before setting her on her feet. But he didn't let her go as he had then. Hands resting lightly against her back, eyelids lowered so that his lashes lay thick and black against his olive skin, he was studying her with an almost painful intensity that lessened the severity of his features, made him look suddenly so vulnerable that hectically she thought, I love him! I really do love him!

The strength of her silent admission made her draw away from him, strangely shaken.

'Where are you going?' He had caught her wrist, his arm fully extended.

'There's a note.' She could see the sheet of white paper through the doorway to the sitting room, from where the evening sun was spilling a red glow out into the hall. 'On the mantelpiece. It must be from Connie.'

Brant glanced lazily over his shoulder. 'So there is.'

But still he didn't let her go.

'I think I'll take a shower,' she murmured tremulously, attempting to tug her hand away, but he just laughed, a soft, low chuckle from deep in his throat.

'Later,' he breathed, pulling her back, those beautiful eyes glittering with something that both terrified and excited her, those proud features flushed with desire. 'We'll do it together. But first, Mrs Cadman, I think we've delayed the inevitable long enough.' Hands on her shoulders now, he kissed her lightly on her forehead. 'I really don't think you should deny it any longer.'

She laughed tensely, the scent of him filling her nostrils. 'Deny what?'

'That this is what you were born for.' His eyes seemed to be stripping her already. 'That you know that as soon as we become lovers, we'll never be able to get enough of each other.'

Because they hadn't made love. During the past two

weeks they had been so busy that he had said he would prefer to wait. When they did come together again for the first time, he wanted things to be unhurried and relaxed between them...

'You scare me,' she admitted guilelessly. 'You're so...experienced and I...I'm not sure what you'll expect.'

He slid his hand along her shoulder, cupped her face in his palm. 'What makes you think I'll expect anything of you? This is about mutual pleasure, darling. Or hasn't it been like that in any of your other relationships?'

Annie dragged in a breath. 'There haven't been any other relationships.'

'You mean...' Brant's eyes were widening in amazement, his hand falling to her shoulder. 'Surely you're not saying...that since we...that there was only ever...'

She didn't answer. She was glad of the fact that since that blazing initiation by him she had had very little time to date, and even less inclination to go to bed with anyone else, and that now her first and only lover had become her husband. But she felt embarrassed by it too, in the light of his hard sophistication, and it must have shown in her face because suddenly he said, 'Don't look so coy about it, sweetheart. I must admit to being a real chauvinist because I'm thoroughly delighted. Unless, of course...' his mouth tugged down on one side '...it was so bad the first time, it put you off for life.'

He had to be joking! she thought, and saw from the humour in his face that he was. Nevertheless, tilting her head, her thick, dark hair burnished with fire from the sunset, huskily she whispered, 'What do you think?'

His eyelids drooped, his mouth drawing down in desire as his gaze embraced the flawless perfection of her throat, the gentle hint of a cleavage beneath the feminine top.

'Show me,' he commanded softly.

Annie's throat ached with the pain of raw need, her fingers longing to touch him, to feel the scary, exciting power of his response.

Standing on tiptoe, she reached up and traced a path down the now roughening line of his jaw, her arms going nervously around him, drawing his mouth down to hers.

He wasn't helping her, she thought as her lips moved tentatively across his, feeling his body like a taut bow beneath her fingers, held in the grip of a tight restraint.

Suddenly, though, he groaned and caught her to him, taking control at last.

'You just don't know how long I've been wanting to do this,' he breathed, when he finally lifted his head. 'Since the second I laid eyes on you that day I came to tell you about Sean, I've dreamed of nothing else since but having you in my bed—and keeping you there—making you sob with desire for me as you did the first time.'

Because, of course, there had always been this between them—this desperate hunger, Annie accepted, even when he had been... But she didn't want to think about that. She, Annie, was his wife now—the woman in his life who was going to love him and please him and drive him delirious for her. Forever and always, she vowed, and, emboldened by the strength of her love, tugged her bodice free of her waistband as he moved to slip it off her shoulders. She shook it off, letting it fall to the floor, and felt his gaze burn across the provocatively low-cut balcony bra it had revealed.

Eager to please him, she had bought the little scrap of nonsense in a very pricey boutique the previous week, unable to resist the coffee and cream lace and silk which now barely covered her breasts.

Brant's breath seemed to catch in his chest. 'Well, well,' he murmured, eyes burning with approval. 'You might be a novice at this, but you've got a siren's instinct for driving a man insane. Do you have any other surprises for me?'

Confident in her femininity now, and her power in what

she was doing to him, she wriggled out of the soft skirt which slid down her thighs and pooled around her ankles, revealing nothing more than a coffee and cream silk G-string and pale, low-heeled sandals enhancing her golden legs.

'You're so beautiful,' Brant whispered in a voice thickened by desire, his taut, flushed features and quickened breathing assuring her of just how aroused he was as she stepped out of the green-gold pool into his arms.

When his hands caressed the soft slope of her shoulders, however, they were surprisingly gentle, their warm strength moving erotically along her upper arms, skimming the outer swell of her breasts, skilfully sharpening her arousal, already heightened by the unexpected thrill of undressing for him.

'So utterly, utterly desirable.' His voice seemed to tremble as he cupped one breast as though it were a rare flower, before pushing the lace aside with his broad thumb and stooping to taste the tantalising pink bud of its tumescent peak.

Annie closed her eyes tightly against the exquisite torture of his mouth, senses sharpening to the sound of his breathing, of hers, to the click of a thermostat coming on in the kitchen, a clock ticking lazily somewhere else in the house.

'I think I'd better take you upstairs,' Brant said raggedly, 'otherwise I might just take you here on the floor, and that's not how I imagined our first time as man and wife to be.'

It was the most incredible experience of her life, from the way he carried her upstairs into the large bedroom with its heavy antique furniture and massive, mahogany-framed bed which he had previously occupied alone, to the way he used his voice, as well as his mouth and hands, to increase her pleasure, leaving her for a moment only to shed his clothes before coming back to join her on the bed, gently guiding her along the mysterious pathways of mutually sensual pleasure.

She had thought nothing could compare with the first time she had made love with him, but now, with his wedding ring on her finger, sure of her position in his life—even if she wasn't so sure of him, she took a greater delight from the licence to wholly enjoy the pleasure he was giving her, felt far less inhibited about pleasing him.

Only when she was sobbing her need, begging for release from this excruciating wanting, did he finally grant it, taking her with him into a spiralling climax of sensation until they collapsed together, and lay sated and sleepy in each other's arms, listening to the gentle burble of the stream.

She awoke to the delicious aroma of cooking, and a day that was unmistakably sunny from the glow beyond the drawn, chintzy curtains.

Languidly she stretched, smiling a soft, contented smile as the movement awakened her to a few tender spots on her body. Brant had shown her ecstasy she had never known existed, she thought dreamily, reluctant to get up. The bed was rumpled, and the air was heavy with the scent of loving.

She was coming out of the bathroom, back into the sun-filled bedroom, wearing only a short silk negligee, having taken a quick shower, when Brant strode in. He was wearing his navy-blue robe, having obviously also showered from the way his hair curled, still slightly damp, at the nape of his neck. But he was carrying a tray and Annie rushed over to see what he had brought up. There were eggs and bacon, orange juice, toast and marmalade, and it smelled wonderful, she thought, ravenous.

'Bed,' Brant commanded, his tone deliciously exciting.

Willingly, Annie complied. 'Aren't you having anything?' she queried, frowning when he sat down on the edge of the bed and was waiting for her to begin.

'I had toast and cereal an hour ago,' he said, watching with approval as she dived wholeheartedly into the mouth-watering breakfast. 'We expended a lot of energy last night. I thought I'd let you sleep.'

She blushed from the reminder. Strange, she thought, how they could be so intimate together and she could feel this shy about it afterwards. But then she couldn't claim to have known him that long yet...

'Is Connie here?' she asked, studying the piece of superbly cooked bacon she had just speared with her fork, oddly embarrassed at the thought of the woman cooking downstairs and guessing why she, Annie, was still in bed.

'Are you kidding?' Brant's tone and expression reassured her on that score. 'She left the fridge well-stocked—that's what she told us in her note—and she'll telephone tomorrow to see if we need anything else.'

'That's kind of her.' Annie felt herself relax. Chewing the bacon, she leaned back against the padded bed-frame and with a slow, smiling appraisal of her new husband said provocatively, 'So you cook as well.'

He didn't say anything, merely dipped his head in wry acknowledgement of her obvious innuendo.

'Are you sure you don't want anything?' she asked when she had eaten and drunk her fill and there was still some toast left, still some tea in the pot.

'I didn't say that.' He was removing the tray from her knees and, with one hand, stretched to place it on top of the dark chest that stood against the wall next to the bed. His eyes, as he turned back to her, were burning with a wicked light, and there was a meaningful curve to his mouth that produced an immediate throb of excitement in Annie's loins.

He reached out and tugged gently at the silk belt of her negligee. The flimsy fabric yielded easily beneath his hand.

Breath suspended, her eyes closing, Annie subsided

against the pillows, letting the garment fall open, body straining towards him in willing offering to his unslaked hunger.

He kept her in bed all day. Not that she had needed much keeping there, she thought wryly when they did decide to get up and she caught a glimpse of the clock. It was five past six! she realised, shamed by her own capacity for love-making.

'It's new. It's natural. It's healthy. No need to be bashful about it,' Brant commented, wise to the colour tingeing her cheeks as she was pulling his robe around her because she couldn't find her own amongst the crumpled bedcovers. 'Come on. Let's get showered and I'll take you out to dinner.'

He drove her to an ancient country inn on the other side of the village, so far off the beaten track that only a handful of locals patronised its rustic and cosy interior.

It was what they had both decided they preferred, rather than driving to one of the more formal and busy restaurants along the coast, and where they indulged in a light meal of ham and cheeses and white crusty bread, washed down with glasses of clear gold wine.

Returning from the powder room afterwards, Annie appreciated the laid-back atmosphere of the place, which meant she had been able to dress ultra-casually. It had been nice simply slipping on a loose T-shirt and short denim skirt after her shower, she thought, wincing as she sat down on the firm-cushioned settle in the quiet corner she was sharing with Brant.

'A little too much loving?' His smile acknowledged her discomfort, as well as the reason for it. 'Perhaps I'd better leave you alone.'

She hadn't intended her response to that to show, but the desire was there in her eyes.

He uttered a self-mocking laugh under his breath, his pupils dilated in the light of the candle that flickered from a glass bowl in the centre of their table. 'If you think I could do that, then I'm afraid you're crediting me with superhuman powers.' His voice was husky with the wanting that even a day's and night's loving couldn't satisfy, and Annie felt an answering need pierce her loins.

Was it natural to want this man so much? To want to reach for him and provoke him into ravishing her here— now—across the table? The idea of it made her legs go weak, caused a sharp contraction at the juncture of her already tender thighs.

'Let's get out of here,' he rasped.

He drove like the wind back through the dark country lanes, his reflexes awesome as he braked sharply once to avoid a startled rabbit.

And suddenly they were there, Annie realised through a reckless, rising excitement, aware of those strong hands bringing the Mercedes onto the cobbled drive, hands which in just a few moments would be driving her delirious with the need to have him inside her again, making her sob for the ecstasy of his possession.

Her tension mounting, she walked ahead of him down the path, watched him put his key in the lock. She thought his hand trembled, but couldn't be sure.

He was right behind her as she stepped inside, one strong arm snaking round her middle, pulling her back against him, even before he had closed the door.

Annie groaned, letting her head fall back against his shoulder. His mouth was almost savage against her throat. His hands were covering her breasts beneath her soft T-shirt, his teeth grazing the flesh of her shoulder, wringing a response from her as desperate as his as he started to rip off her clothes.

'Oh, God!' He sounded almost in despair of his need for her, pulling her round roughly to claim her mouth, making her glory in her power over this man. To have him want her as much as she wanted him was a beginning, wasn't it? Surely he must feel something close to love to want her this much.

'No,' she protested as he made to lead her upstairs, and tugged him after her into the shadowy kitchen, driven by the fantasy that had taken root in her mind back there at the inn.

'I see.' Those two words were strung with sensuality. 'The master-servant-girl scenario, is it?'

Annie blushed. Did he think her wanton? Forward? She didn't care.

'I just wanted to see if my clever, handsome, delectable husband...' she was unfastening his shirt, punctuating each word with a kiss against the deep, dark triangle of hair on his chest '...is as skilful in the kitchen as he said he was this morning...'

'Ah, so that's it,' he breathed in exciting response to the game she was playing. 'Well, my tantalising little wench, I think I can heat something up quite adequately to boiling point, keep it simmering for as long as is necessary, and finally come up with something pretty satisfying.'

His words aroused them both, as they were intended to.

He took her there on the large pine table, her slender hands pinned beneath his, while around them the old beams and timbers groaned and contracted, settling with the night, silent witnesses to the age-old passion of centuries.

CHAPTER NINE

SHE had never been so happy, Annie thought for the umpteenth time since their honeymoon had begun, reflecting on how playful, as well as sensual, her husband could be.

The day before yesterday, after telephoning first, Connie had called round, bringing them fresh strawberries from her garden. It wouldn't have mattered that she had asked if they had been comfortable since they had arrived, Annie mused, if they hadn't all been sitting drinking coffee at the kitchen table at the time. But she hadn't known where to look when Brant, with a sensually amused glance across the scene of their far too recent passion, had captured her gaze and murmured, 'Well, I certainly have been. How about you, darling?'

Blushing to her roots, Annie had watched him enjoying her shamefaced battle to respond normally, but she had had her recompense later in the day.

Strolling along the main beach after nearly everyone had left for the evening, they had found a discarded Frisbee, which they started throwing, running like kids across the sand. That was until a large mongrel dog joined in, leaping through the air and snatching the bright yellow disc before racing off and paddling out into the surging waves, where it decided to abandon it, forcing Brant, in his T-shirt and shorts, to wade in after it.

Thigh-deep in water, disc in hand, he was wading back to Annie waiting on the shore when the wave struck, taking him by surprise and rocking him off balance, so that she was bent double with laughter as he came up onto the beach, his wet clothes clinging to his powerful body.

'So you think that's funny, do you?' he'd said, his tone threatening some delicious punishment, which he evidently meant to carry out, she'd realised when he tossed the Frisbee purposefully back into the sea and made a grab for her, so that she gave a small shriek and darted away. He had caught her, of course, despite all her efforts to escape him, his laughter warm and teasing as he brought her down on the soft sand.

Then yesterday, driving a little way inland, they had found a craft shop selling local artists' work, to which they had returned later with the 'Blue Tit and Poppies' Annie had painted on her last visit, as well as two larger, freer interpretations of the Dorset coast. And then they had come back here to the cottage, talked and read for a while and made love...

Lying now on the settee with her head on his lap, she calculated that they hadn't actually made love for four hours.

Since getting up, rather late, it was true, she had shown him her prowess in the kitchen by baking him a cherry cake. His favourite, she had discovered yesterday, when he had selected it in a tea-shop, only to be told that the previous customer had ordered the last slice. But Annie, after ringing to check on the boys—as they had done every day since leaving London—had gone out while Brant had still been in the shower, bringing back all the ingredients from the village shop to surprise him.

'You shouldn't be doing that—working on your honeymoon.' He had slipped his arms around her waist while she had been stirring the mixture, and gently kissed the back of her exposed neck, where her hair was caught up in a rubber band.

'Why not? I like baking. I don't regard it as work.'

So he had left her to it and they had eaten the cake, still slightly warm, after a king-prawn salad because there had been a fresh-fish van delivering to the village shop when she had tripped light-heartedly down there in the mid-morning sunshine.

Now, replete with food and with each other, they were taking time to relax, and Annie lay gazing up at his dark, arresting features, undeterred because he had discarded the newspaper she had also brought back for him that morning, and was sitting with his head against the cushion, eyes closed, presumably asleep.

He was so incredibly attractive, she marvelled, with her eyes travelling from the corded strength of his throat above his open shirt, to the high sweep of his forehead beneath his black hair. A nose and jaw that suggested forcefulness, she decided, shadowed excitingly dark, that rather cruel mouth—somehow tempered by sleep—holding her in thrall with the knowledge of all it could do to her, so that she was glad he was asleep and couldn't see how hopelessly smitten she was.

But then he opened his eyes and caught her looking at him, gave her an almost distracted smile.

He wasn't asleep, she thought hectically, finding her eyes captured—held by the mesmerising gold of his.

Tell me you love me! she begged silently, not caring any more if he did see the strength of her feelings for him. *I love you!* her heart cried achingly while her eyes searched the mysterious depths of his.

He moved a hand and idly ran his finger along the curvature of her jaw, the tenderness of the action causing her eyes to close from the intensity of her emotions.

You do love me. You do! Say it! Please say it!

She started from the sudden shrill ring of the telephone on the small table just centimetres from her head, felt Brant's body tense, as though in rejection, before he leaned across her.

'Brant Cadman.' His deep, formal tone broke the magic

of the mood, though his chocolate-rich voice alone sent ripples of pleasure through Annie. 'Oh, God!'

'What?' Swiftly she sat up. 'What is it?' Her face was wrought with fear. Sean! Jack! Her mind raced. Something had happened!

'What's wrong?' she pressed urgently. 'What is it?'

Brant put up his hand both to reassure and to silence her. 'It's all right. There's nothing wrong with the boys.'

Annie waited impatiently until he came off the phone. 'There's been a break-in at the house,' he told her soberly.

'Oh, no!' Shamefully, she was torn between relief that it was nothing more drastic and sympathy for Brant, for Felicity. 'Was anything taken?'

He shrugged, picking up the newspaper that had slipped down between them, dumping it down on the arm of the settee. 'Some paintings, a dinner service and some silver. Not the end of the world. But I'll have to go back.'

Annie nodded, understandingly. 'Of course.' She wouldn't have expected anything else. But why had it had to happen? she thought unhappily. They would have been going home tomorrow anyway.

'We'd better make a move,' he said, getting to his feet.

And that was it, Annie realised. Honeymoon over.

It was consolation enough to know both the boys were safe and unharmed, Annie thought as Elise helped her bath them that evening. They had been out with the au pair and their grandmother when the intruders had broken in, and though Brant's initial dread had been what sort of mess they would find on their return, his fears were unfounded. What little disturbance there was had been swiftly sorted out by his staff and it was a relief to discover that decidedly little had been stolen.

In fact, the only one put out seemed to be Bouncer, Annie noted, who must have been lying in his favourite sunny spot on the patio when the burglars had struck, breaking the glass doors and setting off the alarm, because he was slinking around the house now like a cat with a definite grudge.

'Mummy has to leave you with Elise,' she told Sean and Jack when they were back in the nursery, sitting on the window-seat in matching blue pyjamas, drinking their beakers of milk which the young nanny had prepared for them. 'I'll be up to tuck you in,' she promised, giving each of them a kiss, glad to escape the younger girl's company, which was decidedly chillier towards her since she had married Brant.

She had left him downstairs in the study, talking to two policemen. Earlier, someone else had been round, dusting the house for fingerprints.

'Leave it to me.' Brant had instructed when Annie had suggested being there with him to talk to the police. 'It isn't a very nice thing to have to deal with on your honeymoon.'

Smiling over that small consideration, she came across the hall, her soft-soled shoes making no sound on the tiled floor. The study door was ajar so that she could hear the voices. Not the policemen's, as she had expected, just Felicity's and Brant's.

'…Sure that isn't the only reason you're so cut up over losing it Brant?' It was Felicity speaking. 'Telling them you didn't care about the pictures or the—what was it—*damn silver,* just as long as they found your wife's ring?'

Her ring?

Frowning, Annie glanced automatically at the tiny gold band Brant had slipped on her finger four days ago, absently twisting it round with her thumb. She only had one other ring—a silver signet, a present from her parents on her eighteenth birthday—and that was still upstairs in a drawer.

'For heaven's sake, Mother! That wedding ring is all I have of Naomi. *Had!*' Brant's anguished words were like icy fingers around Annie's heart. 'Surely it isn't too complicated to understand.'

'No, but I'm also worried I might understand a lot more than you're telling me.' Felicity's polished tones were subdued in comparison. 'I can't understand why my son had to rush into marrying a second time, without seemingly any thought, any…consideration. It isn't like you to be impetuous, Brant.'

Feeling like an eavesdropper, Annie didn't want to hear any more, but something impelled her, frozen as a statue, to keep on listening.

'Rest assured, Mother, I gave it all the thought and consideration it needed.'

'Did you? And still you married her so ridiculously quickly? Why? Because you didn't want to lose either of your sons? Because you wanted to see them brought up—educated—your way?'

'I hardly think it's anyone else's affair—or right—to question my motives, or my judgement. Even yours, Mother.' That disembodied voice was surprisingly calmer now.

'I'm only thinking of you,' Annie heard the female voice respond. 'And of that poor girl. What did you do? Put pressure on her to see things your way? Persuade her to do what you wanted? You've always been pretty overbearing, Brant.'

There was the sound of a drawer being thrust closed, the squeak of a leather chair.

'I'm sure she would appreciate your concern for her, but give her some credit, Mother. Small though she might be, Annie's no wimp. What are you expecting me to say? I married her because it was the easy option? Because there was nothing else I could do?'

Silence followed, while Annie's heart screamed, *Now*

deny it! Tell her it was because you love me! But, of course, he didn't. Neither did she really expect him to.

'I can't talk to you, Brant,' Felicity said at last. 'Not when you're in this mood. Self-willed and stubborn you might be—and usually that's been to your credit, but I never thought until now I could ever accuse you of being foolish.'

Hearing a movement, realising Felicity was leaving the study, Annie fled along the corridor to the thankfully deserted kitchen, before stumbling through the opposite doorway and up the rear stairs.

An easy option, he had said. Because there was nothing else that he could do! While all the time she'd thought it was because he had some feeling for her. But he had never told her that he loved her. Not even in the most impassioned moments of their lovemaking.

A marriage of convenience, he had told her when he had proposed, but she had wanted to believe that there was more to it than that. But he hadn't told her he loved her, simply because he didn't, and he wasn't a man to prevaricate or lie. A quiet wedding, he had said, with scarcely anyone else involved. She had thought it wildly romantic, so starry-eyed with love that she hadn't been able to see through it to the truth. He had obviously insisted on a no-fuss wedding because he didn't care enough about their union to think it warranted one! Which left her where? she wondered painfully. As just a mother to his two boys and a willing, eager plaything in his bed!

Tears were streaming down her face, even before she reached the top stair. She could hear Elise talking to one of the toddlers in his bedroom, caught Jack's giggling, baby chatter, but she couldn't face anyone at that moment.

It was her lot in life, she decided, making a hasty and silent escape to her old room, always having to come second best with men. With Warren. With the only other boy she had ever had a real liking for, who had given her up simply because he wanted to play more golf!

But this time it was unbearable, she agonised, flinging the door closed, throwing herself down onto the double bed. Not only because she was married to Brant, had given herself to him so completely, shared so many intimacies with him that were shocking now to think about, but because of how much she loved him. The only redeeming factor, she thought, remembering how close she had come to telling him at the cottage that very morning, was that he didn't know.

She had washed her face in the *en suite* basin and had just finished straightening the duvet when a noise outside the room made her glance round.

'There you are!' Brant said, peering round the door.

'Why?' Annie turned away as his smile threatened to dissolve her bones, pulling unnecessarily at the duvet. 'Was I missed?'

He closed the door softly and came up behind her, catching her to him. 'What do you think?' He was lifting her hair, his breath warm and incredibly arousing against the nape of her neck.

Annie sucked in her breath as his hands slid upwards over the tightly stretched cerise of her very feminine top, cupping each of her breasts in his firm, warm palms. Beneath the inadequate protection of her flimsy bra, she felt her nipples hardening in traitorous response.

'What were you doing anyway?' Curiosity laced his words, although thankfully he didn't seem to have noticed that she had been crying. 'Making up your old bed to move back in?'

God! How she felt like doing just that!

'What would you do if I were?' she ventured, trying to contain the bitterness inside of her, then gasped as he pulled her round to face him.

'Are you kidding?' His eyes searching hers, he looked—sounded—incredulous. 'What do you think?' he asked for the second time since he had come in, and with a sensually inspired smile, answered, 'Drag you back to where both you and I know you belong.'

The darkening shadow around his jaw screamed of his virility, and Annie tried not to inhale the scent of his skin, musky from hours driving home, trying to deny the way her body ached even now for the pleasure this one man could give her. Angry with herself, she retorted, 'Back in my place, you mean!' Ignoring the deep cleft that was suddenly knitting his brows, she snapped, 'And where is my place, Brant? Under you?'

Puzzlement gave way to something steely in his eyes. 'From not too distant memory,' he said, 'methinks the lady's more than willing to try it...' He broke off, granting her the freedom she had been struggling for. 'What's got into you, Annie?' His tone was rougher now. 'Have I done something I should know about?'

'I'm tired,' she parried, thrusting her fingers agitatedly through her hair. 'It's been quite a stressful day. I'm sure you'll agree.' Which was better than saying, *I've just found out how much you still love your first wife,* wasn't it? she thought, tortured by the way he had sounded as he'd talked about Naomi in the study.

'Yes,' he breathed heavily.

She shot him a glance, noticing the weary lines around his eyes. Obviously, those hours on the road—because he had insisted on driving all the way back himself—and then dealing with the break-in had taken its toll on him, too. Yet she knew it wasn't just that. It was losing Naomi's ring—the symbol of his love for the other woman—that was making him look so tired, so drained.

'I've got a headache,' Annie uttered, thinking how feeble that sounded, yet it was the only excuse she could think of for adding, 'Do you mind if we don't…I mean…does it matter if we just go to bed to sleep tonight?'

A line appeared between his eyes again as though he didn't wholly believe what she was saying, yet there was a mocking curve to his lips as he said, 'Do you think we can?'

She was aware of him right behind her as she moved over to the door. 'Yes,' she said, catching her breath from his startling proximity as he reached around her, and with impeccable courtesy opened it for her. All was quiet along the landing. The boys had obviously settled down. 'Tonight I will.'

'Then I think you'd better come up alone and leave me downstairs until you're asleep, my dearest, otherwise I'll just be proving to you the fallaciousness of that statement.'

Pain darkened her eyes as she chanced a swift look at him. Oh, how could he, she wondered, anguished, when he was still so obviously in love with someone else?

Without daring to remain there another second, so afraid of disclosing her own reckless love for him, she darted away from him, along the landing, to say goodnight to Sean and Jack.

They spent the next day sorting things out, or rather Brant did. Annie heard him every time she passed his study talking on the telephone, to the insurance company, a locksmith, to the police.

'Leave it to me,' he had said again when Annie, needing something to do, had offered to help him. It might have been to avoid burdening her with it while they were still supposed to be on honeymoon, as he had expressed the previous day, but she had a feeling that there was much more to it than that. It was his and Naomi's home that had been broken into—violated, and from his insistence on doing everything Annie couldn't help feeling superfluous, cast aside, shut out.

Nor did he breathe a single word to her about the ring, although he had mentioned other missing items to her, including some small personal effects of his own, which could only mean one thing, she decided unhappily. That it was far too private, too painful an issue for him to openly admit to her. What other significance could she place on his silence than that?

Eventually, unable to bear it any longer, when he suggested that they slip out for a break from the house that afternoon, and they were driving back from the small hotel where he had taken her for tea, Annie came straight to the point.

'You didn't tell me they'd taken anything of Naomi's,' she attempted to say nonchalantly. 'I mean…anything personal—like her ring.'

She turned her eyes on his lean profile as he brought the Mercedes through a street congested with traffic, but couldn't maintain the contact when he sliced a probing glance her way.

'Who told you?'

Wasn't that accusing note evidence that he hadn't wanted her to know?

'*You* didn't,' she reiterated, keeping her gaze on the rear of a filthy red bus in front.

'No, well…' That laboured sigh wasn't just from having to stop at the same set of traffic lights for the third time in what seemed like as many minutes, Annie was sure. 'It didn't seem…appropriate.'

No, it wouldn't have, she thought poignantly, considering it a cruel twist of fate that the ring he had given his first wife should disappear only days after he had slipped one on her finger.

'Who told you?' he demanded again, much more harshly now.

No one, her aching heart cried. *But if I hadn't found out,*

I'd still have known something was wrong! For what other reason would he have excluded her so completely from helping him sort things out? Appeared so…pained whenever he thought she wasn't looking at him? Because he did. 'I heard you talking about it with your mother last night.'

She felt the questing glance with which he speared her. 'When?'

'I…I don't know. You were in your study.' The bus in front started to rumble forward.

'And where were you?'

'Outside the door.'

'Outside the—' He swore under his breath as someone darted in front of him just as he put the car in motion, leaping onto the bus. 'Why didn't you come in?'

Annie's eyebrow cocked, disappearing under her fringe. Wasn't it obvious? 'It didn't seem…appropriate,' she murmured, deliberately lobbing his own words back at him.

'But perfectly all right to spy on me from behind the door.'

'I wasn't spying,' she snapped, disliking the inference.

'Then why didn't you make your presence known? You're my wife, for heaven's sake!'

'Really?' It was out before she could stop it. 'I was under the impression I was just a…an easy option!'

He shot her a look that was hard, suddenly perceptive. 'Oh, for goodness' sake! That was just something I said because my patience was running out with—'

'Just something you said! Well, I'm glad I know that!' she said, injured, her voice rising.

'What the hell's got into you?' he demanded.

Peering out at the road from beneath her fringe, Annie didn't answer, and as though something had just dawned on him, he asked, 'Was that the reason for giving me the cold shoulder last night?' When she tilted her chin, refusing to give him the satisfaction of a response, impatiently he breathed, 'Annie, for heaven's sake! Surely this isn't all over something you thought I said? Or just because I didn't tell you about losing Naomi's ring?'

Wasn't *all*? Wasn't it enough?

'It was just being reminded that there was someone else. I forgot it for a while. Stupid of me really. But you don't need to explain anything. I understand.'

'No,' he said, putting his foot down on the accelerator pedal as the way ahead suddenly cleared, allowing them to move freely again. 'I don't think you do. If you will go around eavesdropping on other people's conversations…' His gaze, suddenly clashing with hers, forced hers back to the road again. 'Anything you heard between my mother and me bears no relation to anything I feel for you. Or what we have.'

Well, he would say that, wouldn't he?

'I don't believe that you could interpret so much from a conversation you had absolutely no involvement in. Let alone allow this petty jealousy to come between us.'

'Petty? Hardly,' she murmured. 'Not when everywhere I go I feel like an intruder in my own home.'

'I didn't realise that,' he said quietly. Then, in soft, measured tones, as though he was weighing every word, he went on, 'I've been married before. You knew that when you accepted my proposal—agreed to be my wife. I've got a past. I can't help that. But I'm not apologising for it. What's gone is gone. It's up to us now, you and me. But we can't make it work if suspicion and jealousy start creeping into our marriage. Isn't it important to you what we have between us? For heaven's sake! I've never met a woman who could drive me so insane with wanting her. Doesn't that tell you anything?'

Only that where she was concerned, he couldn't help himself, she thought, because even when he had had Naomi in his life that physical force was still there between them,

driving them on into an all-consuming passion that had only
been heightened by its having been so long denied. But it
was only physical, and such fierce, ungovernable passion
could only lead to heartache. As it would eventually, she
thought. As it was doing now. She wanted the love that she
had witnessed in him last night when she had heard him
speaking about Naomi in the study. The ability to touch him,
as losing her ring had, with the agony of despair.

Quietly, she said, 'It isn't enough—what we have. I
thought it would be, but it isn't.'

'That didn't seem to matter to you too much at the cottage.'

Her cheeks flamed from the reminder as he pulled up
sharply again to avoid hitting a car that had just shot out of
a side-turning, ramming his foot down so hard that she
winced from the jolt of the seat-belt across her breasts.

'Nothing to say?' he taunted, when his last statement
brought no response from her. 'Well, I've got something to
say, darling, and you're going to hear it straight. Our marriage might be lacking in a lot of things, but you're darn
well not knocking what it has got. Lie to yourself if you
want to, but don't lie to me. You like having me inside
you—as much as I want to be inside you.'

'Shut up!'

'You want it so badly it dominates everything you think,
say and do.'

'That's not true!'

'Then why exactly did you marry me, darling? Because
it certainly wasn't based on anything like simple, undying
devotion.'

Oh, how could he say that? When he had made it so clear
to her from the outset that this was only to be a marriage
of convenience? It was only her fault if she had allowed
herself to forget that, imagine, like a fool, that she could
make him love her. No one else's.

'You know why.' Though it was excruciating to say it, she pressed on regardless. 'You said yourself it was the only natural solution for the boys. You've got a...convenient mother for your sons and I've got...security...'

'Security?' He was deriding the word before she could add, For them both. 'And whatever happened to honesty and basic trust? Because you can't trust a man, can you, Annie? Any man. I don't know what your relationship with Maddox did to you to screw up that little brain of yours, but it certainly did something! Well, I'm not paying the penalty for it. We entered into a contract—cold-blooded, as you've so carefully reminded me—but a contract nevertheless, in which you agreed to become my wife. And that means honouring that role in full—as I intend to honour mine—for better or for worse. Let's only hope it's for the better. But you've got a lot of learning to do if you're going to throw a tantrum every time another woman's name is mentioned.'

'Another woman...!' She was looking at him, outraged. 'And I suppose you're the one who's going to teach me?'

'This isn't one of our sex games, Annie.' He was looking at her across the confined space, then, shaking his head, he turned back to the road and in a deep, resigned voice murmured, 'I'm not sure I can.'

CHAPTER TEN

THE next two or three weeks passed with a strained politeness between them. Brant wasn't always around during the day—kept busy by his work, and between occupying Sean and Jack, and absorbing herself in her painting when they were with Elise or their grandmother, Annie tried not to dwell on the state of her marriage.

But it was the nights, after they had gone to bed and the rest of the house was dark and deathly still, that they tore down the barriers of reserve that each had erected against the other, communicating in the only way they knew how.

Unlike during their far too brief honeymoon, there were no light-hearted games, no playful laughter to stimulate either of them to arousal. Their relationship, though, strained as it was, had only added a greater urgency to their love-making, a desperation on each of their parts that only heightened the pleasure of their physical coming together in a mutual and almost brutal release.

Almost without exception, however, when Annie awoke, Brant's side of the bed would be empty. Often he had already left the house before she was up, leaving her only with the shaming memory of their lovemaking, and a few sensitive spots on her body to assure her it hadn't all been some shockingly erotic dream.

Cold-blooded was the word Brant had used to describe their passion that day after the break-in, she remembered, shuddering now as she considered that perhaps it was because it had been said that he felt he didn't have to pretend any more. Why then, in knowing how he felt—or rather, didn't feel—did she give him licence to her body, sobbing

151

out her desire, night after night, for the shattering orgasms with him that she craved? Was she warped? Perverted? she asked herself miserably. Did she have such a low level of self-esteem that she could let him use her in any way he thought fit? Without love? Without caring? Perhaps even without respect. Because how could he respect her when, having set out what he expected from her in this marriage— loyalty, truth and, above all, sex, without any emotional commitment, she had not only accepted those terms, but was glorying in them? How could she respect herself? she wondered. And knew the answer even before she had asked it. Quite simply, because she loved him, and so desperately she was prepared to sacrifice anything just so long as she could keep him by her side.

A telephone call from her mother one morning brought the news that Annie had been longing to hear. Simon Talbot was well enough to travel.

'They're going to try and book a flight towards the end of next week,' she told Brant. 'That's if Dad feels he can cope with the discomfort of being so confined for all those hours in the air.'

'Leave it with me,' he said succinctly when she expressed her concern that her father would be all right, which was how her parents managed to arrive exactly when they had planned, just over a week later, travelling in first class and at Brant's expense.

'I never knew flying could be so painless!' her mother enthused as Brant and Annie met them at the airport terminal. 'Wait till I tell the crowd at the sailing club! Brant, I can't thank you enough!'

Looking as chic as she always did with her well-cut, tinted hair and stylish green suit, Jane Talbot, Annie realised as she introduced her parents to Brant, was already captivated by her new son-in-law.

'Jane's right,' Simon Talbot announced, shaking Brant

warmly by the hand. 'I was determined we'd get here as soon as we could, but you've made the whole thing so comfortable for us both. I can't thank you enough.'

'The pleasure's mine, Simon. Jane.' With a totally engaging smile, effortlessly he was hauling their bulging suitcases off the trolley, tactfully declining Simon's offer of help.

'It's no problem,' he said, when the older man demurred that he wasn't carrying anything. 'I'm just saving your energy for the busy schedule Annie's got planned for you while you're here,' he imparted with a lazy glance over her that made her insides quiver, playing down the fact of her father's invalidity, for which Annie—and, she suspected, Simon—was enormously grateful.

Jane gave her daughter a look that said, 'You've done well. I *like* him!' as Brant started off with both cases and a flight bag hanging from his shoulder, and mentally Annie grimaced as her mother quickened her step, catching him up. What was it about the man? she thought, resenting him. Automatically she dropped back, smiling up at her father.

'It's so good to see you,' she breathed, winding an arm affectionately around his. Aided by a stick, he wasn't walking too badly. Just a slight limp, she noted, and there were a few more grey hairs in his sideburns than when she had seen him last.

'It's good to see you, too,' he said, with a wealth of tenderness in that one statement that spoke volumes of the bond between them. 'Only a few more weeks and I'll be as right as rain. It's your mother I've felt more sorry for, having to put up with all the inconvenience of looking after me. She's had to miss out on so much.'

There he was, Annie thought, always considering his kind, but easily flappable wife. 'That's what partners do,' she whispered, her voice cracking with emotion, and had to glance away from those suddenly too discerning eyes.

'So how is he? I mean they?' Jane asked eagerly when they were cruising smoothly back to the house in the Mercedes. She meant the boys, Annie realised, feeling her mother's excitement, her slight nervousness too, over the prospect of meeting her new grandson. 'I just can't get used to the idea of having two grandsons—and I can't wait to meet Jack! Things couldn't have worked out better, could they?'

Which wasn't what she had been saying some weeks ago, Annie thought, remembering her mother's first response to her getting married.

She was sitting beside Jane on the deep rear seat, since Brant had invited her father to join him in the front. Above her mother's excited chatter, she could hear the two men talking quietly together, though she couldn't catch much of what was being said. But then Jane sat forward, leaning through the gap between the two front seats, interrupting the flow of conversation to say, 'You don't know how relieved we are that you took on our baby so that we don't have to worry about her so much any more.' And as Annie sat cringing, she heard her mother adding in a more conspiratorial tone, 'Is she behaving herself, Brant?'

Sitting immediately behind him, Annie met the gold of his eyes in the mirror. Enigmatic, penetrating, they gave nothing away. Neither did his voice as he drawled, 'I've no reason to complain.'

No, she thought, aggrieved, turning to stare sightlessly out at the mellow September day and the already yellowing leaves of the trees in the park that they were passing. I'm meeting your requirements perfectly. By day and by night.

Fortunately she couldn't think any more about that because her father, sensing her discomfort brought on by Jane's over-excitability, turned to tell them about what he and Brant had been discussing, involving all of them, so that they were absorbed in a broad analysis of Britain's involvement with the EEC and its effect on the Commonwealth—particularly New Zealand—for the rest of the journey home.

Her parents' reunion with Sean would have been emotional enough, Annie appreciated, without the added introduction to their blood grandson as well. There were kisses and tears all round, especially from Jane Talbot, who, having accepted the shorter, darker-haired toddler as her daughter's child within minutes, but unable to feel anything but the depth of emotion she had always felt for Sean, couldn't stop cuddling either infant in equal measure.

'How hard it must have been for you, Brant,' Jane acknowledged when Felicity had summoned Elise to take the toddlers, who were becoming tired and irritable from all the excitement, off to the nursery for their nap. 'If you felt anything like we did…finding out that Jack wasn't yours…'

'Mum.'

'I mean—'

'Mum,' Annie cut in nervously, 'and Dad. I've got something to tell you.' Sitting on the pouffe in the elegant drawing room, Annie turned, feeling a light touch on her shoulder.

'I'll help Elise with the boys,' Felicity said softly, the gentle squeeze she gave Annie discreet yet reassuring. She had been delighted when she was told that she was still Jack's natural grandmother as well as Sean's, and though she had voiced understandable reservations, Annie thought, about Brant's hasty marriage that night in the study, that little squeeze just now assured her that she had Felicity Cadman's support, that she was on her side. Ridiculous tears sprang to Annie's eyes and she smiled, warming to her mother-in-law, just as her parents had as soon as they had met this gracious and softly spoken lady who had produced such a dynamo of a son.

Two pairs of eyes were fixed on Annie as the door closed quietly behind Brant's mother. Brant was leaning with an elbow on the mantelpiece, looking as cold and impenetrable as the marble that supported him, Annie noted from beneath her lashes.

'*We've* got something to tell you,' he emphasised smoothly.

But it was her responsibility, Annie thought and, doing what she should have done years ago, uttered, 'It's Jack. He *is* Brant's son.'

Simon's face scarcely twitched, save for the faintest groove that appeared between his eyes. But Jane, suddenly crestfallen and tearful, burst out, 'You mean...he isn't... ours? But you said...' She broke off, trying to comprehend, and Annie thought, Dear God! I couldn't even get that right.

Brant moved away from the fireplace. He looked the only one entirely unmoved, unruffled, in command.

'What Annie is trying to say, Jane, is that when she was pregnant I was the other party to it. Jack's part of both of us.'

Tearfully, the woman looked from Annie to her personable son-in-law, then back to her daughter again.

'You mean...' she was starting to look happier, despite the surprise, her bewilderment '...that the two of you...'

'Yes,' Brant stated, totally unperturbed.

'But how...? When?' The woman couldn't understand why she had been shut out of such an important issue in her daughter's life, and Annie felt for her. Nevertheless, her discomfiture made her respond rather facetiously,

'At a guess, I'd say about two years, eleven and a half months ago.'

'Annie!' Brant's low rasp caught her attention. He made an almost indiscernible movement with his head. He was clearly aware of the tension that too often arose between her and Jane Talbot and was warning her not to incite it.

'Why didn't you ever tell us?' the woman demanded, obviously hurt.

Annie's chest lifted, her breath locking inside of her. Because I was embarrassed, she wanted to say. Ashamed. 'I'm sorry,' she said contritely. She hated having kept it from them. She hadn't intended to deceive either of her parents.

'Why?' Looking deeply wounded, her mother was shaking her head.

'Don't put pressure on the girl, Jane,' Simon, sitting opposite his wife, advised. 'I'm sure she had her reasons,' he said understandingly.

'If it's any consolation...' Brant was addressing both of them '...she didn't tell me either. And yes, she had good reason,' he went on, seeing Jane's puzzled surprise. 'When she found out, I was married,' he admitted, without any holding back.

'Ah,' said Simon, as though he had known all along, while Jane, always going one step too far, bungled on.

'And your wife... Annie said—'

'My wife died,' Brant cut across her, confirming what she already knew.

A tense little silence ensued, but then Simon pushed himself up from his chair and, aided by his stick, moved across to Brant and, extending a hand, said, 'Well, my son, I couldn't be more pleased,' mercifully breaking the awkwardness of the moment.

Her parents stayed three weeks in all, during which time they grew to know their blood grandson, together with the quirks and characters of both the little half-brothers, spoiling them with toys and gifts and all the patient affection of proud and doting grandparents. They enjoyed days out with

Annie and the boys that didn't involve too much walking, bonding well with Felicity, who managed to persuade Jane to accompany her to a couple of her poetry-reading meetings. Then there were the days when they all went out together as a family unit, when Brant joined them, which always seemed to be the most enjoyable and exciting for the boys, and for everyone else, Annie couldn't help thinking.

Then there were the times when, aware of Simon's interest in modern building design and architecture, Brant took the older man along to look at some of the Cadman developments in progress, inviting Simon's ideas and opinions, so that Annie could see a natural and mutual respect deepening between the two men, for which she could only be grateful.

By the end of their stay, Jane looked much more relaxed, and Annie was pleased to see that her father's walking had improved, and that he had more colour in his cheeks than when he and Jane had arrived.

'Try not to expect too much from a partnership,' Simon told Annie when they were strolling in the garden already touched by autumn. Gold leaves trespassed on the damp, yet still immaculate, regularly raked lawns, and a chilly breeze heralded the end of September—and her parents' departure. They were leaving the following day and Jane had gone with Felicity to get her hair styled, ready for the trip home. 'If you expect too much you can sometimes forget to give and you'll always be disappointed. It's about giving as well as taking in equal measure. Never forget that, Annie.'

No, it isn't. Not with you and Mum, she thought, but she didn't tell him that, wondering, as she tucked her arm into his, if Brant had said anything to him, or if, with that quiet shrewdness of his, her father merely suspected that there was something wrong with her marriage.

They saw her parents off the following morning, having

taken them to the airport. Then, almost in silence, Brant drove Annie home. The boys had said their goodbyes at the house, after which Felicity and Elise were taking them to the zoo, so that the place was strangely quiet when they returned, which didn't help Annie's feeling of loss now that her parents had left.

She headed straight upstairs to hide the sudden wave of emotion that overcame her as she saw on the hall table the little pot of purple chrysanthemums that her father had bought her earlier in the week.

Powdering her nose, she was relieved to be back in control by the time Brant came up. He didn't say a word, but she was conscious of him moving around the wide double bed, opening a drawer, crossing to the dressing room and the *en suite*.

He hadn't made love to her during the whole period of her parents' visit. Perhaps his conscience would have pricked him too much, she thought grudgingly, using the daughter of a man he so obviously respected with nothing other than pure lust while that man was under his roof.

She was straightening from picking up an old luggage label from one of her parents' cases that had been lying by the dressing table, and glanced up as Brant came back into the bedroom. He had changed from his casual wear into a dark suit. She remembered him mentioning he had a board meeting that afternoon.

'It's quiet,' he commented, stooping to adjust his tie in the mirror.

'Yes.' Looking at his reflection, Annie noticed how beautifully sculpted his hands were, how sinewy and strong. Drained with emotion, she murmured, 'Thanks for being so nice to Mum and Dad.'

Surprise widened those equally beautiful eyes. 'How else would you have had me be?' he asked, turning round now.

'They're nice people. It wasn't too much of a hardship being nice to them.'

She didn't answer, swallowing the lump in her throat, feeling his eyes on her as she studied the crumpled label, dropped it into the wastebasket.

'Come here,' he said softly, gently.

Her feet seemed to have lead weights on them as she moved over to him, seemingly against her will. And she thought, Why am I doing this? Because I want him to hold me? Kiss me? Make love to me?

Nothing could prepare her for the rush of desire as his arms went around her, and when his lips descended on hers every need of every female for her man down through the centuries seemed to invade her body. Abstinence, it seemed, had only played its cruel part in helping to enslave her so that she was greedy for him, all pride obliterated, her self-respect lost, as his mouth devoured hers.

She was wearing scarlet linen trousers with a matching linen top thrown over a pale camisole and he made short work of dispensing with them all.

In only her cream bra and G-string, she gave an inward sob of despair at herself as he picked her up, carried her over to the bed, needing him, wanting him more than she had ever wanted anything. And he was oh, so exquisitely tender.

But he hadn't undressed, she realised through the heady torture of what he was doing to her as he tossed aside her lacy bra, nor did he attempt to, seeming to want nothing but the pleasure his lips and hands alone could wring from her body.

When he sat up to peel off the fine triangle of her G-string, she reached out, clutching at the soft fabric of his suit.

'No,' he whispered when she would have drawn him down to her, instead shifting his position to kiss that most intimate part of her, and with such unbearable ecstasy that a small, guttural sound left her throat.

His hair was a sensual caress against her sensitive skin as wave upon wave of sensation held her in breath-catching rigidity. The world receded and spun, setting her free on a dizzying spiral of pure rapture until the contractions of her body throbbed away, leaving her damp and sated and still.

He was still fully clothed, still immaculate apart from his hair, which was no more than slightly tousled. Swiftly then he moved, drawing the heavy white bedspread up across her nakedness.

'I'm going away,' he said. 'After the meeting this afternoon.'

Annie sat upright, clutching the thick, cool bedspread to her heated flesh. 'Where?' she queried, frowning, alarmed.

'Geneva. I've got something in negotiation over there. It could take some time, but I need to be on hand.'

Then can't I come with you? The boys and I? she wanted to say. We could do with a holiday. But he'd have asked her if he had wanted her with him, she reminded herself painfully, and so all she said was, 'Oh?' And, sounding unemotional, 'How long do you think you'll be gone?'

He shrugged. 'Three weeks. A month. Long enough for you to enjoy the joys of motherhood without the inconvenience of a husband. After all, isn't that what you want?'

How could he say that after what had just happened between them? she wondered achingly, but like him she shrugged and said, 'If you say so.'

They both glanced towards the window, hearing a car coming along the drive. Felicity returning with Elise and the boys, Annie realised, seeing it register with Brant too, before he turned and went back into the *en suite*.

'Be good,' he breathed, bending over her with a fleeting brush of his lips across her forehead just a matter of minutes later. Then he was gone, leaving her with only the lingering scent of his cologne.

Dragging herself into the shower, Annie stood under the steaming jets, hoping the water would ease her lethargy, her sudden extreme tiredness. But then she always seemed to be tired these days.

It had to be the strain, she decided, letting the warm water cascade down over her body. The strain of loving a man who wasn't in love with her. Well that was just her own fault for being conceited enough to have imagined a man like him could ever love her, she thought, still dwelling on the subject as she switched off the jets and reached for a bath sheet. She'd known the facts before he'd slipped a ring on her finger and yet she still...

Patting herself dry in the fluffy green towel, Annie frowned down at her left hand.

Her ring! Where was it? She had scarcely taken it off since the day Brant had given it to her, but it wasn't there now. So where was it? she wondered hectically. Had she taken it off? Put it down somewhere without thinking?

Wrapping the bath sheet around her, she raced through into the bedroom. A quick scan of the dressing table, however, proved futile, as did a swift survey of the floor and an even more thorough search of the bed.

Think! *Think!* she urged herself desperately. When had she seen it last? Certainly she had been wearing it that morning when they had taken her parents to the airport. And then, coming back, Brant had had to make an unscheduled stop at the motorway services so that Annie could use the bathroom. Had she taken it off then? Put it down on the basin while she had washed her hands?

She couldn't believe she would be that careless. She treasured it, and had always been very circumspect about putting it down. All she could remember was the hand dryer in those services not being very effective, and wiping her hands on her trousers as she had made her way back to the car. Her ring was always a little loose when her hands were wet. Had it come off then—in that car park? Was it lying there even now, being driven over by unsuspecting motorists? Or would somebody have picked it up? Put it in their pocket, unable to believe their luck?

She dropped down onto the bed, her shoulders slumping. Her husband didn't love her. He was going away, so that she wouldn't have the inconvenience of him being here, was what he'd said. And now losing her wedding ring only seemed to emphasise the fragility of her marriage.

She spent the next couple of days feeling dreadfully under par. Not unwell exactly, just very tired and a little bit nauseous. Which was all due, she decided, to lying awake for hours each night, going over the problems of a marriage that had seemed to start so well and which now seemed to be going so terribly wrong.

That Brant wanted her physically was without question, that driving desire for her every bit as intense as hers for him. But a man could have a woman like that while still loving someone else, she reminded herself painfully, while the female of the species was prepared to sacrifice all her pride and dignity for the love of just one man.

She wondered where he was now. In one of the ski resorts probably, which he had said he was moving on to when he had telephoned last night, mainly to enquire after the boys. Well, if he wanted to act so cold and uncaring, then two could play at that game, Annie had thought miserably, and had kept her answers to his cool, emotionless questions clipped and matter-of-fact. And if he *had* rung off sounding curt and offhand, then it served him right, speaking to her in that brisk, businesslike tone!

The voice that had wounded her so much over the telephone, though, didn't quite equate with the man who had made love to her so tenderly and unselfishly only minutes before he had left, and she wondered why he had. Probably to keep her wanting him all the time he was away, so that when he returned she would still be the dutiful wife and mother. In other words—firmly in her place!

Even so, the anger and hurt that surfaced as she reminded herself of how 'convenient' she was to him couldn't prevent the tight band of desire that seemed to wind itself around her body as she thought about that last day, or the shaming knowledge that if he were here now he would only have to reach for her and she would be lost.

She spent the next few days organising some new frames for several of her recent paintings, liaising with Brant's solicitor over the pending sale of her flat, and accompanying Felicity on a trip into town.

'Have you heard from Brant?' the woman wanted to know when they were indulging in a light lunch in the restaurant of the famous Knightsbridge store.

'Yes,' Annie said, toying with the delicate pink flesh of her poached salmon salad, and didn't know what else to say. *He rang once but we were so cold towards each other, he hasn't bothered since?* 'He was keen to know how the boys were,' she tagged on quickly, because not to enlarge would have seemed odd.

'You're looking a bit off-colour.' Felicity's warm eyes were studying her daughter-in-law solicitously.

'Am I?' Affectedly, Annie laughed. She didn't tell Brant's mother that she wasn't sleeping or eating properly either, or that Katrina had said exactly the same thing when Annie had met her the last time at the gym. 'Late night,' she bluffed with another forced chuckle, which was the wrong thing to say, she realised, when the woman frowned almost imperceptibly, her gaze falling to the table as Annie reached for a portion of bread roll.

'My ring? I must have left it in the bathroom,' she pre-varicated, viewing her splayed fingers, unable to tell her mother-in-law that she had been careless enough to lose her ring. In truth, though, she had tortured and berated herself terribly for doing just that. She had even driven out to the motorway services the day she had discovered it was missing, searching the car park for the unlikeliest chance of finding it; enquiring at the information desk just in case anyone had handed it in.

'Are things all right between you and Brant?' Felicity was still looking concerned.

Annie swallowed, nodded. 'Yes, of course,' she answered, dry-mouthed, because how could she say anything else?

'You haven't had a quarrel or anything?'

No, of course not. Not a quarrel. Just that my husband doesn't love me! He still loves Naomi, and I can never hope to compete against that!

Annie shook her head. 'No. As you said, I'm just a bit off-colour,' she admitted with a fleeting smile to try and divert Felicity's interest away from her very private problems. She was glad when the woman responded similarly, sitting back on her chair.

'I'd just like you to know, dear...' that genteel diction, instilled in Felicity by the family who had abandoned her—abandoned Brant—was threaded with sincerity behind the cool refinement '...I had my doubts about the two of you marrying so quickly. I was worried for Brant—and for you. But now...' she lifted a napkin to her mouth, having finished the creamy mound of grilled goat's cheese she had ordered '...I think you can only be good for my son, Annie.'

A waiter brought them coffee, the thick, strong aroma that drifted towards her as he poured it making her stomach churn in sickening revulsion. Quickly she jumped up and, murmuring some excuse to the other woman, fled to the cloakroom, where miserably she gave in to the nausea that overcame her.

It was Sean's sudden shrieking that made Annie glance up from where she was sitting, sketching in the mellow October sunshine, only half-aware until then of the baby chatter and the strongly accented voice of Elise coming from behind the high hedge.

Abandoning her sketch, Annie leaped up to investigate the tantrum, guessing that it was probably over Sean being denied his own way than anything else.

She had reached the bronze statue when the French girl emerged through the gap in the hedge, clutching the red-faced, unhappy Sean by the hand.

'Sean. He find this,' Elise explained in response to Annie's initially concerned query. 'Down behind the bushes.' She was holding out a white supermarket carrier bag. 'It was fastened in…how you say?…a knot…and I…' The girl gave a careless shrug.

She had obviously untied it, Annie noted, puzzled, taking it from her, nursing a secret relief that she wouldn't have to suffer Elise's cool attitude towards her for much longer, because the girl had only that morning handed in her notice.

The bag was soiled and there was a light chink of some-thing metallic as Annie pulled it apart to peer inside.

. 'No. Maman, she must have it,' Elise was saying to Sean, who was still crying, trying to grasp the bag, while Jack came toddling noisily up behind them. 'We go inside now, yes?'

As the young nanny trundled away with the two protest-ing infants, Annie's dumbfounded gaze returned to Sean's find. It contained a man's watch, obviously an old one of Brant's, some gold cuff-links and a rather expensive-looking tie-pin. Things that had been taken during the break-in, Annie realised, subsiding onto the seat beside her. Perhaps whoever had taken them had dropped the bag or perhaps hidden it in the bushes until they had finished loading the paintings and other items that had been stolen. Perhaps they had been planning to come back for it and had been disturbed.

There was something else too, lodged in one corner of the bag, and Annie knew what it was even before she drew it out.

The ring that had caused Brant so much anguish to lose.

Lying on the palm of her left hand, the deep gold of the metal shone richly in the low sun, and Annie couldn't help comparing the ring with the fading narrow band of white flesh around her third finger—almost blended with her skin tone now that her summer tan had also faded, as though a ring had never been there. The one Brant had given Naomi was altogether wider, richer, bolder, making the precious slim band that Annie had chosen and lost seem like a pale, insignificant trinket in comparison.

There was an inscription inside and she held it up between her thumb and forefinger so that she could read it more easily.

For Eternity. That was all it said, but its significance sent a dart of pain through Annie.

It seemed like a cruel twist of fate, she thought, that she should lose her own ring only to find Naomi's, especially when her husband hadn't even been home in nearly a month, and only ever telephoned to ask about his boys. Everything, it seemed, since she had met Brant again, was trying to tell her one thing. She had no right loving this man. He belonged to another woman—he always had. If she had had a living rival, then she might have known how to handle it, but she didn't know how to fight a memory, a predecessor whose influence was everywhere, in this house, these gardens. Over Brant...

Silently, beneath the cold, pitiless bronze of the statue, she sobbed out the hopelessness of it all.

CHAPTER ELEVEN

RINGING Brant's mobile phone and only getting his voice mail, Annie left a text message instead.

Items of jewellery recovered this morning. Found by Sean in bushes. Then, unable to help herself, she had tagged on, *Got your wife's ring.*

He didn't respond that night, but the following morning, groping for her phone on the bedside cabinet, as Annie had half expected, an answering text from him popped up on to the display.

Good for Sean, she read, deciphering his abbreviations. *We'll make a detective out of him yet. And Annie—in case you've forgotten—you're my wife.*

But only in name! she thought poignantly, tossing the phone down onto the bedspread. He hadn't even bothered to tell her where he was, or when he might be coming home!

Fortunately, this morning she was feeling better so she didn't linger in bed, grateful to shower before the boys were up and about.

Coming downstairs, she found a letter addressed to her on the hall table and took it into the deserted drawing room. Bouncer jumped up onto her lap when she sat down to read it, paws kneading, purring loudly.

It was from the little shop in Dorset. They had sold her four paintings and enclosed a cheque with a request for more of her work if she had any to sell.

A wave of longing washed over her, so strong it made her catch her breath. Down there in that cottage where she had spent her brief honeymoon, everything had promised to be so perfect—so right. If only they hadn't had that break-in, she thought, torturing herself, absently stroking Bouncer's soft, feline fur. If only she hadn't overheard Brant talking about it in the study, heard the anguish in his voice when he had lost the only thing that seemed to matter to him. But that depth of feeling he still harboured for the woman whose shoes she had tried to fill would have manifested itself in some other way, sooner or later, she realised achingly. Oh, if only she didn't love him so much!

But it was no use dwelling on what might have been, she berated herself, feeling the cat settling down, fighting the emotion locked like a painful vice in her chest. She had a family to bring up, as well as a living to make, and she'd start by taking some more of her paintings down to that shop. She wouldn't waste any more time crying over spilt milk—or even jelly! she thought, grimacing at Bouncer, steeling herself against the cruel reminder of how Brant had proposed to her after that particular incident. And she'd do it right now. Determinedly she lifted the instantly protesting cat off her lap. Today!

The shop's proprietor was pleased with the four full-sized water-colours with which Annie supplied him, bolder replicas, loosely painted as before, of the red headlands and magnificent chalk cliffs she had photographed back in the summer.

'No other artist seems to capture the mood of our landscape quite like you do,' he told her, missing the sadness in the small, casually clad woman whose work he was appraising. 'They've got such soul.'

And heart, Annie thought, touched by his comments, struggling with biting tears as she left the shop. She knew she could never have produced them if she hadn't been so in love with the man who, for her, represented everything about this daunting and spectacular coast.

Having left the boys back in London, she was all set to

turn her car for home, when suddenly nostalgia proved too great for her. She was so close, it wouldn't hurt just to pop into the cottage, would it? She would only stay a few minutes. But Brant's country retreat was like a living thing to her. She just couldn't come here, could she, without paying her respects?

The pale stone building stood dreamily in the late-October sunshine, and there was such a strong sense of homecoming as Annie opened the front door, stepped into the little lobby, that she realised instantly that she was wrong to have come.

Oh, what a fool she was! she thought achingly, moving through into the sitting room. Today would only create more memories to torture her along with all the rest.

There was a newspaper lying open on the arm of the sofa. The one Brant had been reading that last morning they were here, she remembered, the sight of it piercing her to the heart. They had left in such a hurry that day, they hadn't even bothered to move it, she thought, picking it up and carrying it through to the kitchen without even sparing it a glance, not wanting to be reminded of the topical things they had talked about while she had been lying there, so happy, with her head on his lap.

Only the large refrigerator hummed in the companionable silence. Purposefully, Annie crossed over to the swing bin beside it and, gritting her teeth against a ridiculous sense of loss, dropped the newspaper inside.

Why was she thinking of keeping it as a souvenir? A souvenir of what? she wondered bitterly. Of something that had never been? Something in her own mind? A mere illusion?

Letting the cold tap run, she filled the electric copper kettle and switched it on. She had stopped on her way there to buy milk and tea bags, and she had brought some cheese biscuits too. Having little appetite, she had passed up the idea of buying a sandwich. Some biscuits though, she had decided, would help stop the nausea if she should suffer an attack while she was out.

Listening to the singing kettle, she reminded herself that there was something else she needed to do. But not yet, she thought, putting it off while she dropped a tea bag into a mug, poured on the boiling water.

She noticed that the wooden bread box wasn't properly closed and moved over to shut it. Something made her push up the concertina lid. There was half a small wholemeal loaf inside. It wasn't green, just very, very stale, she realised thankfully, taking it out and depositing it in the swing bin with the newspaper, wondering why Connie hadn't thrown it away when she had come in to clean after their last visit, and guessed that the housekeeper might not have thought to look in the container until restocking it before they came again.

Carrying her mug across the kitchen, she fished out her tea bag by its string before dropping that into the bin also.

Brant's presence was everywhere, she thought, sipping her tea after pouring on milk from the open carton behind her. If she closed her eyes she could imagine she could smell his aftershave lotion impinging on the air, hear his almost silent footsteps coming through the lobby, feel the dominating weight of his body as he made love to her there...

'Brant!'

As if her aching heart alone had conjured him up, he was standing in the doorway on the other side of the old pine table.

'Annie?' He sounded as shocked as she was, though he must have noticed her Ka parked outside.

Carefully she put down her mug, wondering why she hadn't heard him drive in. 'What are you doing here?' It was almost an effort to speak.

'I was going to ask the same thing of you.'

He strode into the room, moving lithely for his build in a dark casual shirt and dark corded trousers, dropping keys and a carrier bag down onto the table. Groceries, Annie noted. From the village store.

'I wasn't staying,' she blurted out, because it was evident that he was. 'I—I brought some more paintings down to that shop we found. They'd sold the others.'

'Great. Well done. Congratulations.' Trite clichés, as if he didn't really know what to say.

'I thought you were in Switzerland,' Annie said, biting her lip.

'I was. I got back yesterday.'

'You didn't come home.'

'No. I had to see a client in Bournemouth. When I got back here last night, I'm afraid I just slept and slept.'

Which was why he was out shopping late for groceries. On foot, she decided, guessing that his car must be in the garage. She noticed now, though, the dark circles under his eyes and how lean he looked—leaner than when she had seen him last. Worriedly, she wondered if he had been over-working; why he hadn't simply booked into a hotel.

Tentatively, she asked, 'Why did you come here?'

He slipped his hands into his pockets. 'Why did you?'

Why had she?

'I told you. I was in the area. I felt like a cup of tea.' Not, *I wanted to see the place again. To remember what it was like. What we shared...*

'Not to take a look at the old place? Just for old times' sake?' he enquired cynically, and much too near the truth.

'No.' Annie gripped the sink behind her, unintentionally drawing his eyes to the gentle curves of her body beneath her thin purple sweater and khaki trousers. 'I just needed to rest for an hour or so. I just thought I'd check that everything was all right here.'

'Likewise.'

'What was he saying? That he wasn't avoiding her?

'The boys missed you.'

'I missed them.'

But he wasn't saying he had missed her.

'You don't look very well,' he observed.

Neither do you, she thought, considering that hungry leanness about him. His stripping regard of her pinched features was disturbing, however, and Annie shrugged, answering coolly, 'I've probably been pushing myself too hard.' Then, keen to change the subject, 'You got my message,' she mentioned cagily. 'About the stuff Sean found?'

'You know I did.'

'Aren't you pleased?'

'Delighted.'

Well, he would be, wouldn't he? Even if he didn't particularly sound it.

He was still looking at her with an intensity that made her throat ache, and she turned away, saying quickly, 'Would you like a cup of tea?'

He hesitated as though he was about to refuse. Then, with his breath seeming to leave him in a rush, he said, 'Thanks. There's some bread in the box if you're feeling peckish, and I bought some...'

Bread? In the box? 'I thought...' Annie wasn't listening to what he was saying he had bought. 'I mean...' She pointed to the pine container now standing empty on the worktop. '...Wasn't that left over from last time we were here?'

Brows drawing together, Brant crossed over to the oblong box, flipped up the concertina top.

'I'll admit it felt like a brick when I put it in there last night...' Mildly mocking, those green-gold eyes scanned the worktops.

'I threw it away,' Annie admitted, feeling like a fool.

She could sense his eyes on her as she reached for a mug

from one of the wall cupboards, picked up another tea bag, flicked down the switch to reboil the kettle.

'All that I had to sustain me from sure starvation and without a second thought my wife casually jettisons it.' He was being flippant, she realised, until he said, 'Where's your wedding ring, Annie?' Then his quiet observation almost made her spill the boiling water she had started to pour from the kettle. 'Have you jettisoned that, too?'

How could he ask that? Tears made her eyes burn, but she carried on with her task, keeping her head down so he wouldn't see.

'I don't know. I don't know where it is. I lost it—in the services, I think, the day we dropped Mum and Dad off.' How casual, how unaffected she managed to sound!

'Why didn't you tell me?'

'What good would it have done? Anyway, I didn't realise until after you'd gone…' Remembering those last moments with him and how tender he had been caused an ache in her chest that almost made her gasp. Her shoulder lifted slightly beneath the purple sweater. 'I hoped I'd find it first without having to admit to you that I'd been so careless.'

Careless. Nonchalant. That was how she appeared, she thought, knowing that if she dropped the façade she would break down completely.

'Then we'll just have to get you another one, won't we?' he stated phlegmatically.

A sob almost tore from her throat. *No, I wanted that one!* she wanted to cry out. *You don't know how much it meant to me. But you don't care because it doesn't hurt you the way it did when you thought you'd lost Naomi's!*

'Here's your tea,' she told him quickly, pushing the mug towards him before grabbing her bag that she had deposited on one of the kitchen chairs and racing upstairs.

He was pacing the sitting-room floor when she came back down some time later.

'I was about to come looking for you.' His eyes were narrowing as they made a swift assessment of her. 'Are you all right?'

She felt drained, washed-out, but she shrugged and said, 'Of course I am.'

'You've been ages.'

Because she had been trying to bring her raging emotions under control. And because it had taken that long to do the test.

'You look ghastly,' Brant remarked, his forehead furrowing as he studied her pale, tense features, the slightly blotchy skin around her eyes.

'Thanks. It's always nice to have a man compliment you,' she answered, stuffing her hands into her back pockets.

'Don't be facetious.'

'And don't worry your head unnecessarily. I'm fine.' His mug was on the low table beside the sofa, its contents only half-consumed. 'Finish your tea. Sit down. Relax.' Her tone was clipped and breathy. 'I'm sorry to disturb your peace but I'll be going in a minute. In the meantime…' she pivoted round to go back to the kitchen '…just pretend I'm not here.'

'That's rather difficult to do.'

That sudden wry comment curtailed her progress. Was it? Did she disturb him that much?

Colour touching her pale cheeks, she turned round, forcing herself to remember that there was only one way in which she disturbed this hard, red-blooded man, warning herself not to be a fool.

'And as far as relaxing goes…' He was picking up one of the large cushions on the sofa, tossing it down again '…perhaps I would if I could find my paper.'

'Your paper?'

'Yes, it was there.' He gave a jerk of his chin towards

the arm of the sofa. 'Yesterday's *Telegraph*. Open at a double-page article I was reading.'

'I thought…'

He looked at her askance. 'You thought what?'

Annie trekked through into the kitchen. God! Why couldn't she have left his things alone?

Without her being aware of it, he had followed and was standing right behind her as she fished the newspaper out of the bin. There was a big brown stain spreading outwards from the tea bag that was stuck to the article he had been reading. And she had thought it was the paper they had shared when they had been so happy here together. When she had imagined it would only be a matter of time before she could make him love her.

Hormones running riot, tears suddenly sprang from her eyes and she couldn't make them stop.

'Annie. Annie! What is it?' He was pulling the unfortunate paper from her grasp. 'For heaven's sake, Annie! It's only a tea bag!'

She flinched from his hand on her shoulder, backing away against the table, needing its steadying solidity for support.

Sobbing angrily, she burst out, 'I'm not crying over a tea bag!' She heard the bin-lid swing as he dropped the newspaper back inside.

'What, then? What is it?' He was moving back towards her. 'Annie, please. Come on, sweetheart. Tell me.' Both hands were gripping her firmly by the shoulders now.

His expression was so concerned, so deceivingly caring that she couldn't look at him. Loving him as she did, she couldn't bear it, pressing her eyelids tight against their dark-circled wells so that she wouldn't have to see his reaction as she sobbed hopelessly, 'I'm pregnant.'

So was the pause, she decided after a long, long moment and, opening her eyes, she realised it was because he was too shocked to speak.

Mercilessly, his gaze raked over her tired and strained features, over the tears streaming uncontrollably down her pallid cheeks. Soberly and very quietly then he said, 'I see.'

No, you don't! she thought. *You don't see anything. Not how much I love you! Not how much this marriage means to me! You don't see a thing because you're so wrapped up in the past!*

'I'm sorry it happened. But we haven't exactly been very careful, have we?' she threw at him bitterly. 'And don't tell me to get rid of it because I'm not going to! I'm keeping it and I don't care if you don't want it! I do!' Roughly she pushed his arm away, swinging round to stare out of the small-paned window. The garden looked as nature intended, bright with autumn, leaf-strewn, a wildlife haven. Tight-lipped, she saw that there were cobwebs clinging randomly to the old yew hedge that ran around the property, dew-speckled, fragile as mist.

Gently but determinedly, Brant was turning her back to face him. 'What makes you think I wouldn't want it?' he breathed, looking amazed.

'Because it ties you to me even more!'

His lips moved in almost mocking indulgence. 'And you to me.'

'It isn't me we're talking about, is it?' she challenged, sniffing, groping in her pocket for a tissue. 'I don't care about that.' Impatiently, she checked the sleeve of her sweater. 'I want to be married to you.' There, she had said it. Now let him pity her for all he liked—use her admission to salve his ego if he wanted to! God! Where was her tissue?

He was striding across the kitchen. To get some kitchen-roll, she realised as he tore off a sheet. Now he was opening one of the small pine drawers of the dresser, closing it again, his movements so familiar to her, so unbearably dear.

'Here,' he said, coming back to her.

Gratefully, she took the square of patterned paper from him. It felt rather coarse as she blew her nose.

He studied her for a few moments while she composed herself, then very gently he caught her wrist, lifted her left hand.

'My ring!' she gasped, astounded, as he slipped the slim gold band on her finger. Eyes shining from more than just her tears, she looked up at him questioningly. 'Where did you find it?' She couldn't stop looking at it. She couldn't believe that she had got it back.

'It was on the floor of the car, behind the passenger seat. I didn't see it until yesterday when I picked the car up from the airport and I was putting something in the back.'

'It must have slipped off after I'd come out of those services,' she said, thinking aloud, 'because my hands were still wet...' Then with all the emotional upheaval of seeing her parents off, and the tense hour or so afterwards when they had been driving back, she hadn't realised. And after that, of course, they had made love... 'It's funny, isn't it?' she murmured with something like a heavy weight pressing down on her as she remembered. 'That all along you've had mine and I've got yours.'

'Mine?' he queried, baffled, dropping a glance to the very masculine ring she had given him on their wedding day.

'Well, Naomi's,' Annie corrected. 'Yours and Naomi's.' Just like with our babies, she realised. A cruel, ironic switch-around.

'What are you talking about?' The sun, shining through the window, streaked his hair with fire. A deep groove was knitting his black brows.

'Her wedding ring. The one that was stolen. Or which you thought had been stolen,' she amended brittly. 'The one you were so cut-up about. That you seemed to think I was being so unreasonable over when you didn't tell me. OK. Maybe I was. Maybe I have been. I tried not to mind.'

'Mind?' His hands shot out on either side of her, trapping her between the sink and his disturbing proximity when she would have moved away.

'That you still love her,' she uttered, answering the hard question in his eyes. 'That I was only ever second best.'

'Annie...'

'I've tried to be reasonable and tell myself that of course I am. That I wasn't the person you'd have chosen to spend your life with. Not really. Not if—'

'Annie. Annie.' His deep, firm voice held an edge of exasperation. 'I thought you knew. I thought you understood. I haven't wanted to... God help me! It hasn't been easy, but perhaps it's time I made you understand.'

A tilt of his head gestured for her to precede him into the sitting room.

What was he going to tell her? That, of course, she had to be reasonable. What did she expect? He had been married before. He had told her that once—that he wasn't apologising for it. Nor, she thought, for how he still felt. She knew she couldn't expect him to stop loving Naomi. Or to expect to step into her shoes. She just didn't want him to spell it out to her—that was all.

From the sofa, on the edge of her cushion, she watched him pacing in front of her.

'Sometimes,' he began, 'sometimes I've thought it's all been one long punishment for marrying someone when I knew I was in love with someone else.'

'Brant—' *Don't,* she had been about to whisper, unable to bear hearing whatever it was he had to say, but he put up a hand to stop her. *Let me go on,* it said. The line between his eyes and the clench of his jaw told her how painful it was for him. She looked away from him, down at the rug, seeing the browns and greens and ochre weave swim before her eyes.

'We'd been seeing each other for a long time—Naomi

and I. It wasn't the fierce, uncontrollable thing that we have. It was easy. Uncomplicated. Comfortable. I suppose you could have called us little more than occasional lovers. I made no commitment to her—or she to me. I thought that was the way she wanted things. I certainly didn't question her feelings—or mine—for anything beyond that. And then I saw you. You were with Maddox at the time, but something sparked between us that a thousand fiancés couldn't have prevented. I knew I couldn't have you, but the stirring you caused in my blood assured me of one thing. That what I had with Naomi wasn't—and never would be—enough.'

Frowning, Annie raised her head. What was he saying? Breath held, she listened more intently and with growing wonder as he went on. 'We went away for a weekend as we sometimes did and I decided to tell her from the outset that I thought we should finish our relationship—that we were being unfair to each other carrying on with something that clearly wasn't going anywhere. She didn't seem to mind. She was always very practical. Down to earth. Sometimes, I used to think, a little too unemotional. Like that beautiful cold statue she had imported from Florence.'

So that was what he had meant when he'd said it reminded him of her. And she'd thought… But it didn't matter now what she'd thought, Annie decided, trying to grasp—take in—all she was hearing.

'I wondered afterwards if it was all an act. Playing it cool because that was how she imagined I wanted her to be. We made love for old times' sake—her words, not mine,' he uttered drily. Hearing Annie catch her breath, he added, 'I'm sorry. I didn't want to have to go into such detail, but I have to tell you. We parted as we always had. As casual lovers. Undemanding friends. But this time it was for keeps.

'Five weeks later I went to that party and there you were—but without Maddox this time. I knew you were on the rebound, but when you came on to me as you did, I was knocked sideways. Shocked. Surprised. Flattered. I knew it wasn't the right time to get involved with you, but my darling, you were far too irresistible to leave that night. I wanted you in my bed—in my life—and I was so afraid of losing you, I must confess to taking advantage of your vulnerability. But the next morning when I woke up, you'd gone. By the time I rang your office on the Monday morning, you'd already left, and your old boss told me you'd gone abroad. I couldn't believe it—that you'd leave just like that. I felt as though I'd been slapped in the face. Told myself I was being stupid. You were merely a young woman I'd spent a very pleasurable night with, I kept telling myself, but I knew there was much more to it than that. You'd got under my skin like no other woman I'd ever known and it didn't do any good reminding myself that I was a grown man. That I was thirty-two and head of a successful and thriving company. I was determined to wait for you to come back—no matter how long it took—and woo you properly, make you see how right it was what we had together. But then just over a week later, Naomi rang and asked to see me urgently. She was at home, she said, and she sounded dreadful. I drove over there and I'd never seen her so desperate—so wound up. She told me then that she was pregnant. That it should never have happened as she was taking the Pill. I wanted to bury my head in the sand—pretend that it wasn't happening—but I couldn't do that. This was my child. A child I was responsible for as much as she was. She was crying as she told me about it.'

Just as she had been, Annie thought, out there in the kitchen.

'I didn't think she wanted marriage. That she ever loved me. But then she let it all out. That she'd pretended she didn't care, because she'd been afraid that I'd reject her if I'd known that she was serious. That she didn't know what she was going to do. That, strong and independent as I believed her to be, she couldn't cope with a child on her own. We were married several weeks later, and I tried to make the best of it. I didn't realise until afterwards that it was Naomi being helpless that was the act. It wasn't until a few months later, presumably thinking I was happy, that she told me. She'd stopped taking the Pill to try and get pregnant on purpose because she'd known I was losing interest. I couldn't believe it when she told me it had happened on our last weekend together.'

So Naomi had effectively trapped him into marrying her, Annie realised, shocked, sympathising with him. Surprisingly, though, she felt a degree of pity for the woman who had dreaded losing him enough to have acted that desperately.

'I felt unbelievably angry. Hurt. Betrayed. And then she died having Sean.'

Having never held him, Annie remembered. And then there had been that mix-up. Sean had come to her, as good as fresh from Brant's arms, and Jack they had simply handed over to his rightful father.

'When she died,' he went on, 'I thought I was being punished for feeling as I did—and for my crazy infatuation, as I thought it was, with you. When I found out there had been a switch, that not only had they given my son away but also who he was with, I couldn't believe such a coincidence could happen. I'm not superstitious, but I felt as though I was being punished—until I saw you again, and all I wanted to do was hold you, comfort you and try to spare you the pain of hearing what I had to tell you.' He came down beside her, caught her to him, his shuddering emotion evident in his voice as he murmured, 'I just wanted—needed—you, so much.'

Annie gasped from the joy of being in his arms. He smelt so musky and familiar to her, and his body was so warm and strong. 'But you never told me how you felt.' Her eyes were shining as she lifted her head from his shoulder. She couldn't believe he was saying it now. In a minute she would wake up and discover that it was all a dream. A big, beautiful, unbelievable dream!

'I didn't think you'd believe it if I did. It was all so soon. And I thought you were still carrying a torch for Maddox, or at the very least holding a grudge against men because of what he did to you. I didn't want to do—or say—anything that would make you turn tail and run.'

'But ever since we've been married, you've never once told me how much you cared. I thought you still wanted Naomi. That you'd just married me because it was the most convenient thing to do. For the boys. That's what you said.'

'Did I?' He rolled his eyes in a self-deprecating manner. 'Sweet Annie.' His face was lit by tender warmth now. 'Did Maddox destroy your self-esteem to such a degree that you thought a man couldn't value you for yourself? Oh, I'll admit I used the boys' welfare as a lever to persuade you to marry me, but I knew it would take a lot of tenderness and understanding before you let yourself go in another full-blown relationship, and I didn't want to run the risk of losing you again in the meantime. I love you,' he breathed openly at last. 'Couldn't you see that?'

She could. Of course she could. It was there in his eyes, in his voice, in the warmth of desire she could feel enveloping him, enveloping them both. But, puzzled, she asked, 'Why didn't you tell me all this—about Naomi—before?'

'She's my son's—Sean's—mother,' he reminded her. 'She was also very insecure to do what she did. I didn't want to say anything detrimental about her.'

'You didn't,' Annie reassured him. 'You merely told me the truth.' And then, remembering something, frowning, she said, 'Is that why you were so upset when you thought her ring had been taken? Because you thought you were being punished again for not feeling as you thought you should?'

Surprisingly, he laughed. 'Good heavens, no!' he responded. 'Of course. That was how this all started, wasn't it? No,' he was stressing surprisingly again. 'That ring wasn't a symbol of *our* marriage. It was her grandmother's and, I believe, her great-grandmother's before that. Naomi was orphaned at an early age and that ring was the only heirloom she possessed. I don't know how she managed to come by it, but she treasured it as the only link between herself and the family she had never known. I wanted it for Sean—or rather Jack, when I thought he was hers. It's the only thing I can give my son from his mother's side of the family.'

'And I thought…'

'Yes, I know what you thought—now.' His tone was gently admonishing. Tenderly then, he took her left hand, was fondling its delicate structure with his broad thumb. 'I was more worried when I thought you didn't care about losing yours.'

'Of course I cared! I was beside myself,' Annie admitted. 'I even went back to the services in the hope of finding it. Is that why you didn't tell me you had it immediately? Because you thought I didn't care?'

'Could you blame me?' he challenged. 'I was beginning to wonder if you felt that you'd simply been bullied into marrying me when you really didn't want to be with me at all. I know Mother accused me of that,' he said, reminding her of the conversation she had overheard in his study. 'Perhaps she could see how unhappy you were when I couldn't.'

'I wasn't unhappy—being with you. Only feeling that I was only second best. But I do want to be with you. I would have come with you to Switzerland if you'd wanted me to. I could have brought the boys along. I was longing for you to ask me, but you didn't.'

'Oh, Annie,' he said. 'Have we been a pair of perfect fools?'

'Fools.' She smiled now. 'Only not so perfect. Oh, Brant! We can try again, can't we?'

'I think, my darling...' he held her at arm's length, dropping a glance to her still very sleek middle '...we've tried and succeeded. Carry on like this and we'll soon have our own five-a-side soccer team.'

'Hey, steady on! Three's quite enough to begin with. Although, who knows?' she added, with a mischievous twinkle in her eyes. 'Just as long as their mother's never again made to feel that she's a substitute!'

He laughed at her play on words, but then, more soberly, he murmured, 'Is that how you felt?'

'All along. Right from the day I came back from France and Katrina told me you were married. I didn't think I could tell you about our baby anyway, but when I realised you'd married Naomi—I knew for certain I never would. I thought then that I'd been just someone to amuse yourself with even though you were really serious about *her*, and I was so crazy about you. You'd always scared me to death—or how you affected me did anyway. When I went to that conference with Warren, where I saw you that first time, I really thought I was happy with him. But from the moment you first looked at me, I think I started to have doubts. Although I'd been so hurt by him and still felt so dreadfully humiliated that night of the party, after we made love I didn't feel a thing for him any more. All I could think about was you. For days and weeks afterwards. Then when I found out I was going to have your baby...'

'I love you,' she whispered, reaching to trace the firm, slightly abrasive line of his jaw.

Angling his head, he kissed her very softly on the corner of her mouth, so softly in fact that her love for him sprang as tears to her eyes. Sniffing them back, she glanced down at the tight, crumpled ball in her hand.

'Just a minute,' she laughed nasally, and darted off to the

kitchen for more paper towel, yanking at the unsuspecting
roll. It spun round on its holder, releasing its pretty patterned
sheets, which just kept coming and coming and coming.

A strong masculine hand slammed down on the animated
roll.

'You're a disaster,' Brant breathed, amused, tearing some
off for her.

'I know,' she admitted, burying her face behind handfuls
of paper towel. 'I told you. It's the way you affect me. I
couldn't even hang on to my own baby.'

He laughed softly under his breath, his arms going round
her. 'That,' he said, 'was a deliberate ploy by our joint des-
tinies to make sure that one day I'd come looking for you.'

'Oh, Brant...'

'And stop crying,' he advised, smiling, 'or it's going to
cost me a fortune in paper towel.'

Dark hair moving softly against her shoulders, Annie
laughed up at him through her tears. 'Take me to bed,' she
whispered, her voice husky with emotion.

A long time later, lying in the deep mahogany-framed bed
in the crook of Brant's arm, she murmured wistfully, 'I suppose I'd better be getting back.'

'We,' Brant amended, in a way that made her heart leap.
'I'm not letting you out of my sight again unless it's absolutely necessary.' Moving to prop himself up on an elbow,
he gazed down to where she lay, flushed and dishevelled in
the sweet aftermath of their lovemaking. 'You aren't happy
there, are you?' he remarked sagaciously of his London
home.

'If you're there, I will be,' Annie told him, promising
herself she would adapt to his lifestyle. 'It's just that I feel
a bit out of place amongst all that stern elegance and formality.' She smiled apologetically, closing her eyes as Brant
dipped his head to place a tender kiss on her nose.

'Because it isn't you,' he murmured. 'That's why I brought you here to begin with. I thought it would be more suited to your uncomplicated, candid nature. I didn't want to watch it become gradually more and more stifled by what I can only see now as a place that belongs to the past, and that will never be able to give you all the natural, simple things in life that I know you're looking for. It wasn't until you were there with your carefree spirit and meeting with all those delightful calamities that I realised how unfriendly my home was. I felt ashamed of it,' he concluded.

And she'd felt inferior—displaced! Annie thought, amazed.

'We don't have to live there. We can sell the house,' he was telling her, already making plans. 'Mother wants to go back to Shropshire to be nearer her friends anyway. But we can live anywhere. Here, if you want to.'

'Can we? Oh, Brant!' She flung her arms around him, her head turned into the warm, musky velvet of his shoulder. 'This place suits me so much better because the walls aren't straight and the rooms feel like part of the garden, and it doesn't matter if someone drops beetroot all over the floor.'

'You're right. It suits you,' he chuckled. And then more seriously, 'But not for any of those reasons. But because it's easy and unpretentious and welcoming, all the things you are and I don't deserve to claim for myself. That's why I came here last night. To try and recapture the magic of what we had. Or maybe it was to torture myself, I don't know.'

Sighing, she nodded in understanding, felt his arms tighten around her, and knew, without even telling him, that he understood that the same reason had prompted her to come too.

'I'll try and make you happy, Annie,' he breathed, 'if you don't mind spending your life with a man who's so in love with the only woman he's ever wanted to be married to, he can't see straight.'

Held tightly in his arms, she felt the emotion shudder through him.

'If you don't mind spending your life with a wife who you've said yourself,' she laughed, 'is a disaster!'

A sound of approval rumbled from his throat. 'It'll make for an interesting and exciting lifetime. Especially if you promise me that I can claim some forfeit for every bit of chaos you create in my life.'

'What did you have in mind?' she murmured suggestively, feeling the stirring heat of desire rising in her again.

'Oh, this…' his lips were teasing on her neck '…and this…' now across her shoulder, sending shivering little thrills along her spine.

'In that case…' her brown eyes, dark with desire, were lit by a spark of wickedness '…I must confess to having dyed your best shirt orange. Well, speckled orange, actually. The cat's clawed your grey suit. And wasn't it that beautifully bound encyclopaedia in the walnut bookcase that used to be your favourite?'

She was making it all up, instigating this game of provocation and payment, and he knew it, but still he was responding. He always responded, she thought, aware of his own surging desire, which was what made it all so wonderful, so perfect.

'You should have told me before. Then I could have taken everything into account. As it is…' playfully, he caught her wrists above her head, holding them in one hand, leaving his other hand free to roam '…you're just going to have to settle with me for each separate issue.'

'And then?' she whispered.

'Then we'll go back to London. Put the house on the

market along with your flat. And then we'll pack up the boys and that sulky cat of yours and bring them home.'

Home. As his lips and hands caressed her, she stole a covert look up at the crooked ceiling, heard the burbling stream, saw the golden glow the low autumn sun was casting over the walls. She would always be grateful to this house, she thought, for drawing her back when she might have driven home and left Brant here, as unhappy as she was, still misunderstanding, still tearing each other apart. But because they had come back they had found each other, had a real home, an understanding, a beautiful future.

In the cooling day the old beams settled, seemed to give a sigh of satisfaction.

Thank you, Annie mouthed secretly—fondly—to them, and then gave herself up to the fire of mutual passion.

If you enjoyed what you just read,
then we've got an offer you can't resist!

Take 2 bestselling
love stories FREE!
Plus get a FREE surprise gift!

HARLEQUIN *Presents*

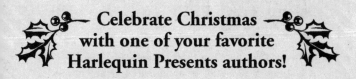

Celebrate Christmas
with one of your favorite
Harlequin Presents authors!

THE SICILIAN'S CHRISTMAS BRIDE
by Sandra Marton

On sale November 2006.

When Maya Sommers becomes Dante Russo's
mistress, rules are made. Although their affair
will be highly satisfying in the bedroom,
there'll be no commitment or future plans.
Then Maya discovers she's pregnant….

Get your copy today!

SAVE UP TO $30! SIGN UP TODAY!

INSIDE *Romance*

The complete guide to your favorite
Harlequin®, Silhouette® and Love Inspired® books.

✓ Newsletter ABSOLUTELY FREE! No purchase necessary.

✓ Valuable coupons for future purchases of Harlequin,
  Silhouette and Love Inspired books in every issue!

✓ Special excerpts & previews in each issue. Learn about all
  the hottest titles before they arrive in stores.

✓ No hassle—mailed directly to your door!

✓ Comes complete with a handy shopping checklist
  so you won't miss out on any titles.

- -

SIGN ME UP TO RECEIVE INSIDE ROMANCE
ABSOLUTELY FREE
(Please print clearly)

_____

Name

_____

Address

_____
City/Town   State/Province   Zip/Postal Code